D0783448

A son.

He had a *son*.

The words hammered inside Gus's head, and for several moments all he could hear was the rushing of blood in his veins as it pulsed with a matching rhythm…a son, a son, a son, a son.

A shiver of reaction ran down his spine. As he struggled to control the welling of emotion that brought an uncharacteristic sting to his eyes he felt the light brush of Holly's fingers on the back of his hand. Without conscious thought he gratefully accepted the physical contact, moving so they were palm to palm, their fingers naturally interlocking.

'My s-son,' he asked, stumbling as he voiced the word aloud for the first time. 'How is he?'

'He's a fighter. Given the trauma of the accident and the delivery—and the suggestion that he could be up to four weeks premature—he's in miraculously good shape. So far,' Mr Haggerty informed them.

Relieved despite the words of caution, Gus expelled a shaky breath. 'Thank God.'

Dear Reader

Welcome to Strathlochan and the tenth of my loosely-linked Scottish stories—my fourteenth Mills & Boon® Medical Romance™. Unfortunately, this book has taken many more months to come to fruition than expected, due to a prolonged spell of illness which prevented me from writing. After the heroic efforts of the real-life doctors, nurses and support staff at my local cottage hospital—to whom I send my heartfelt thanks—I've been able to return to my fictional heroes and heroines at last.

With two of her closest friends, Gina and Ruth, settled with their respective partners, it is Holly's turn to find love. She's waited a long time for her happy ending. So has Gus. They had something special, and lost it before their love had a chance to blossom, but sometimes life rights past wrongs and grants second chances. Fate intervenes to bring Gus and Holly back together, uniting them in a common cause. Can the hurt, resentment, betrayals and misunderstandings of the past be resolved? And will Gus and Holly finally enjoy the happiness they both deserve?

There are more Strathlochan stories waiting in the wings, and I hope I'm well enough to bring them to you without such a long wait in between. Whether you've visited the folk in Strathlochan before, or this is your first time, I hope you will enjoy Gus and Holly's emotional journey and come to love them as much as I do. I also hope you will return to Strathlochan again in future. I'm looking forward to introducing you to Rafael and Georgia in the next story. For now, though, the stage belongs to Gus and Holly…

Love

Margaret

www.margaretmcdonagh.com

margaret.mcdonagh@yahoo.co.uk

BROUGHT TOGETHER BY BABY

BY
MARGARET McDONAGH

First published in Great Britain 2012
by Mills & Boon, an imprint of Harlequin (UK) Limited.
Large Print edition 2012
Harlequin (UK) Limited, Eton House,
18-24 Paradise Road, Richmond, Surrey TW9 1SR

© Margaret McDonagh 2012

ISBN: 978 0 263 22472 6

Harlequin (UK) policy is to use papers that are natural, renewable and recyclable products and made from wood grown in sustainable forests. The logging and manufacturing process conform to the legal environmental regulations of the country of origin.

Printed and bound in Great Britain
by CPI Antony Rowe, Chippenham, Wiltshire

Margaret McDonagh says of herself: 'I began losing myself in the magical world of books from a very young age, and I always knew that I had to write, pursuing the dream for over twenty years, often with cussed stubbornness in the face of rejection letters! Despite having numerous romance novellas, short stories and serials published, the news that my first "proper book" had been accepted by Harlequin Mills & Boon for their Medical Romance™ line brought indescribable joy! Having a passion for learning makes researching an involving pleasure, and I love developing new characters, getting to know them, setting them challenges to overcome. The hardest part is saying goodbye to them, because they become so real to me. And I always fall in love with my heroes! Writing and reading books, keeping in touch with friends, watching sport and meeting the demands of my four-legged companions keeps me well occupied. I hope you enjoy reading this book as much as I loved writing it.'

www.margaretmcdonagh.com

margaret.mcdonagh@yahoo.co.uk

**Praise for
Margaret McDonagh:**

'The romance takes a sensual turn
that will have readers longing for the
couple's much deserved happily-ever-after.'
—*RT Book Reviews* on
VIRGIN MIDWIFE, PLAYBOY DOCTOR

With special thanks to:

Dr Nick Edwards, author of *In Stitches*,
for help with my research

John and Jennifer,
for all your help and kindness

Fiona, Craig, Jackie, Lesley, Irene, Fiona,
Janet, Gwen, Caroline, Christina, Maggie,
Pam, Wolfie, Anne, Richard and Fiona
for being there for me

Jo—editor *extraordinaire*—
for your support, patience
and encouragement

All the staff at the local sanatorium,
aka The Madhouse!
Words are insufficient to thank you for
everything you've done for me,
in so many ways,
and for all your kindness and care

CHAPTER ONE

'You won't believe this, Gus, but the air ambulance is on its way in.'

Dr Gus Buchanan glanced up from the notes he was writing as Carolyn, the nurse assigned to assist him, returned to the treatment cubicle after seeing out their most recent patient. *'Again?'*

'Again,' Carolyn confirmed, her tone and wide-eyed expression echoing his own incredulity.

The warm and sunny June day should have been unremarkable, but he was eight hours into his shift and Strathlochan Hospital's A&E department had been bedlam for every minute of it. The chaos showed no sign of abating: every treatment cubicle was in use, the emergency phone continued to ring non-stop, and now the air ambulance, which had already responded to a record number of calls since early morning, was back in action once more.

Gus snapped the file closed and pocketed his pen. 'What the hell is going on today?'

'Heaven knows. It's the craziest shift I've had in the five years I've been here,' his colleague informed him, shaking her head. 'How many patients have we treated and sent home?'

'I've lost count.'

'Me, too. And the Minors waiting area is *still* full to bursting. They're at breaking point in Resus, too, and have already called in off-duty staff to help. If it carries on like this I wouldn't be surprised if they had to call for more.' As she talked Carolyn busied herself clearing up the debris he'd left after stitching a pensioner's nasty leg wound. 'The helicopter must be attending something especially serious, Gus, because Kathleen all but threw the emergency phone at Laura in Reception before rushing off to alert Robert Mowbray. I've never seen her that upset before.'

Nor had he. Gus frowned. The fact that Kathleen O'Leary, the unflappable department manager, was acting so out of character highlighted the unusualness of the day, but it was hearing how overstretched his colleagues were that increased his frustration. He'd spent the day stuck in Minors rather than being in the thick of the action as part of a Resus team. All the doctors rotated round the A&E department and, whilst he generally enjoyed taking his turn in Minors—where he had more time and saw a wider variety of patients—it was the adrenalin rush of emergency medicine that called to him, testing his skills and giving him the buzz on which many trauma doctors thrived.

As Carolyn washed her hands and applied antibacterial gel to them before setting about restocking the dressing trolley, Gus slid off the high stool he'd perched on to write the notes and stood up. 'While you prep things here, I'll find out what's next on our agenda.'

'OK, Gus.'

He didn't admit it aloud, but he was secretly hoping that Robert Mowbray, the head consultant on duty, would notice him and reassign him to help out in Resus, despite the queues in Minors.

'Thanks, Carolyn. Grab yourself a cup of tea when you're done.'

His suggestion earned him a rueful smile. 'The chance would be a fine thing! No one has stopped all day, yourself included, and I can't see any sign of that changing.'

'Not if the patients keep coming at the same rate,' he agreed, masking his fatigue, knowing it was shared by all his colleagues.

Caroline sent him a quick grin. 'One of the registrars has dubbed today Wild Wednesday.'

'Let's hope it doesn't turn into Tempestuous Thursday and Frantic Friday, too,' Gus countered, returning her smile.

'Don't even joke about it!'

Carolyn's chuckle followed him as he left the cubicle and negotiated his way along the busy corridor. She was a pleasant and competent young woman to work with, Gus reflected. All the nurses were. Apart from department vamp Olivia Barr, whose professional standards left much to be desired and whom he avoided whenever possible. But neither Carolyn nor any of the other nurses was as naturally skilled or as instinctively on the same wavelength with him as Holly had been.

His step faltered.

Holly…

For a moment the breath caught in his throat as

everything within him tightened and his mood darkened. Holly was the nurse with whom he had become so close following his arrival in Strathlochan the previous August. Now even thinking about her was forbidden and upsetting—although that didn't stop his mind lingering on her far more often than he cared to admit. Holly had burrowed into his psyche and, try as he might, he hadn't been able to banish her.

Things between Holly and himself had turned sour suddenly and in so many ways that it had been both a relief and a wrench when she had transferred to the Children's Ward at the beginning of the year. He'd refused to acknowledge or unravel his own complex responses to her leaving. But there was no doubt that A&E had lost one of its finest nurses...or that his colleagues held *him* responsible for that loss.

A distinct chill had lingered in the atmosphere after Holly's departure. Support and sympathy had lain squarely with her, while he had universally been dubbed the villain of the piece. The truth? It *was* his fault. And no one knew that more than him. Although it didn't absolve Holly of blame for her own part in things, no one felt more guilty, more angry or more riddled with self-disgust and regret than he did, and no one could think less of him than he thought of himself.

He'd been a loner all his life. It had never bothered him. Indeed, he felt most comfortable behind the barrier he put between himself and the rest of the world. Only when he'd been plunged back into the self-inflicted spell of isolation after the events with Holly had he fully realised how much of a difference she had made, how much she had changed him, and how much colour she had brought to the greyness of his world.

Through Holly he'd had a taste of acceptance and friendship and belonging the like of which he had never experienced before. Until, following her rejection of him—which had hit hard when he'd been at his lowest ebb—he'd thrown it all away in a moment of weakness. Through his own stupidity he'd lost any chance of reconciliation, of persuading Holly to change her mind about taking their relationship to the next level and, as a result, his hope for a promising future with Holly had been shattered.

Yes, Holly had played a part. She'd hurt and

disappointed him. And finding out that she'd kept things from him, that he hadn't known her as well as he'd thought, had dented his trust in her. But blaming her didn't excuse his own reaction, and feelings of guilt and self-disgust continued to torment him.

Since Holly's transfer from A&E he'd kept his head down and worked hard, more grateful than he'd expected to be when, as the days and weeks passed, he had slowly won back the professional acceptance and co-operation of his colleagues. What they thought of him personally was less clear. He only knew that self-respect remained a long way away.

Since the chasm had opened up between them he'd been careful to keep his distance, and once Holly had moved to the Children's Ward he'd gone out of his way to avoid running into her around the hospital. He hadn't caught even the briefest glimpse of her for weeks. Unfortunately out of sight had not rendered her out of mind. Holly continued to haunt him, which not only irritated him no end but added to the disappointment, confusion and hurt he still felt at the slightest thought of her.

And, above all, the pressing weight of guilt.

He had no business whatsoever thinking about Holly. Not any more. Not since the night when her public rejection of him had sparked off the chain of events that had rollercoastered out of his control, culminating on the day in December when his mistakes had come home to roost.

The day of his hastily arranged civil marriage.

The day Holly had become his sister-in-law... and Julia his wife.

Gus bit down the derisive, humourless laugh that rose inside him. He used the term *'wife'* in the loosest sense of the word. Not that anyone had a clue about the true state of his six-and-a-half-month marriage. Which was just the way he wanted it. Apart from the man who had been his mentor throughout his troubled teenage years—a man whose premature death four years previously had left a big and painful hole—there was only one person in whom he had truly felt able to confide anything about himself and his life.

Holly.

And now she was the one person he could never talk to again—especially about his sham of a marriage to her sister Julia, and the loneliness he felt within it. The situation was entirely his own fault, and no matter how difficult things were all he could do was make the best of them. Because within the next few weeks the dynamics would change again and he would have a new role. A role he had never planned on or wanted and which brought with it a whole new range of frightening emotions and responsibilities: fatherhood.

As he approached the main desk the charged atmosphere and tension within the A&E department became even more evident. Robert Mowbray was talking intently on the emergency phone, while Kathleen was busy keeping up with the instructions Robert fired at her.

'What's happening, Laura?' Gus asked, handing the young clerk the patient file on which he had just signed off. To his surprise, the normally bubbly and talkative girl shook her head and avoided meeting his gaze. 'Are you OK?'

'Fine.'

The response was muffled and the girl's head remained bowed. Clearly she was anything *but* fine. Making a mental note to keep an eye on her, Gus moved to the nearby whiteboard. As he wiped off the details of his last patient he listened in to Robert's side of the conversation, and it was immediately obvious that Carolyn had been right: something major *was* taking place.

'I trust your judgement, Frazer,' the consultant said, identifying the caller as Frazer McInnes, one of the flight doctors on Strathlochan's air ambulance. 'Kathleen is calling in the relevant specialists and alerting the operating theatre now. She may have experienced the first signs of labour before the crash… No, I agree with you. Our primary concern has to be for the baby and making every effort possible to save it. If she wasn't wearing a seatbelt she might have sustained such fatal injuries hitting the steering wheel and the windscreen. How's the foetal heartbeat? I'm not surprised the baby's showing signs of distress. Do what you can to control the haemorrhaging. We're on standby ready for you. We'll bypass Resus and go straight to Theatre.'

Gus suppressed the wave of nausea that ripped through him as the horrific implications of the accident sank in. How dreadful for the casualties—the pregnant woman's family in particular—but his sympathies also went out to the medical personnel. Any emergency that involved a baby was always difficult but, like himself, Frazer was also anticipating becoming a father soon, so this would be painfully close to home right now.

He certainly didn't know how *he* would cope were he in Frazer's place, confronting such a critical, challenging and emotional situation, Gus admitted, a shiver running down his spine. This was one occasion when he was glad to be in a well-equipped A&E department with back-up at hand rather than dealing with the pre-hospital conditions out at the roadside, making the best of what was available and taking the responsibility of making split-second life-and-death decisions.

Robert hung up the phone and turned to address the assorted personnel who were gathering around him and who seemed, Gus thought, more tense and edgy than usual. Why were they acting so strangely? Even the department's joker, registrar Dr Will Brown, renowned for his ready smile and sense of humour, was uncharacteristically sombre and subdued. Puzzled, Gus put his colleagues' changed behaviour down to the stress of the incredibly busy and pressured day.

'ETA four minutes. I need extra fluids made ready—Frazer will be running low,' Robert announced, and a senior nurse hurried off to do his bidding. 'Kathleen, ask Security to help maintain a clear route to Theatre. And alert the blood bank. A transfusion is more than likely.'

'I'm on it.'

Hoping to make himself useful, Gus stepped closer, but when he caught his boss's gaze he was unable to read the expression that lingered there before the older man turned away to issue further instructions.

'This is a unique and horrible situation, so focus on your tasks and not on the wider implications,' he advised cryptically, puzzling Gus further. 'You know what to do. Let's get on. Someone hold the lift so there's no delay when we need it. Kathleen…?'

'Security are on the way. I've notified the blood bank. And I've fast-bleeped the emergency obstetrician and neurologist. They're going straight to Theatre to scrub up,' the middle-aged woman announced, the waver in her lilting Irish voice and her unusual pallor increasing Gus's concern and the insidious feeling that something was very wrong here.

Grim-faced, Robert nodded. 'And the neonatal consultant?'

'He's dealing with a problem baby in Paediatric Intensive Care next door,' Kathleen explained, referring to the maternity wing adjacent to the main hospital. 'But he'll be across directly.'

Unsettled, Gus spoke up. 'Is there anything I can do to help, Robert?'

'No!'

Gus was taken aback by the shrill and sudden denial—even more so because it came from Laura. A flash of anguish in her own eyes, Kathleen hurried across to the girl, who was clearly distressed.

'Take a break in the staffroom to get yourself together,' the older woman advised, kind but firm. As Laura pushed back her chair and hurried away, Kathleen exchanged another pained glance with Robert. 'I'll talk to her when I've finished here.'

'Of course,' the consultant agreed.

Before Gus could query Laura's strange reaction, Robert laid a hand on his shoulder and drew him aside.

'Gus…' He paused and shook his head, concern and compassion evident in his eyes before his gaze strayed towards the entrance. The doors were open, allowing them to hear the first sounds of the approaching air ambulance. 'Please wait for me in my office,' Robert continued. The distinctive noise of the helicopter's rotor blades increased as the aircraft descended onto the landing pad. Gus was aware of Robert's hand tightening briefly on his shoulder before contact was withdrawn. 'I'm sorry, Gus. I'll come and talk with you in a few minutes.'

The consultant was rushing through the department before Gus could ask what he was sorry for and what he wanted to talk about. As he made his way to the office his unease increased in unison with the strange buzz in the department. If Robert wasn't going to reassign him, he needed to get back to Minors to see his share of the patients requiring attention. Either way, he didn't want to be cooling his heels here for long.

His thoughts took an abrupt change of direction when he saw Frazer McInnes enter the department at a run, his flight paramedic Rick Duncan at the other end of the stretcher. Both men were covered in blood and carrying IV lines in one hand while guiding the trolley with the other. And both looked drained, clearly shaken by the traumatic events they had witnessed at the accident site and on the flight to the hospital.

'Clear the way!' Frazer called, his voice rough and impatient.

As Frazer, Rick, Robert and their entourage rushed down the corridor to the lifts, Gus offered up a plea for the baby's survival. Moved by the tragedy, he thrust his hands into the pockets of his scrub trousers and paced the small office, too on edge to wait patiently. He was on the point of returning to Reception to question Kathleen when his boss returned.

An inexplicable shiver of dread rippled through him at the uncharacteristically bleak expression in Robert's eyes as he entered the room and closed the door behind him.

'Sit, please,' he invited.

Gus did as he was asked, but instead of moving round the desk to take his own chair Robert stood beside him, once more resting a hand on his shoulder. Rather than reassuring him, the gesture increased Gus's unease. A dark premonition chilled his blood.

'What is it, Robert? Have I done something wrong?' he asked, unable to bear the electric silence another moment.

'No. No, of course not,' his boss responded, sounding weary and resigned. 'Gus, there's something I must tell you…'

Holly Tait finished the scheduled observations and wrote the information on her six-year-old patient's chart. The little girl had returned from Theatre less than twenty-four hours ago following an operation to remove her infected appendix. Understandably, she was still very sore. Holly checked the chart to see when the next medications were due, her disobedient gaze straying to the signature of the A&E doctor responsible for the girl's admission.

Gus Buchanan. Pain lanced through her, but Holly knew that hers, unlike her patient's, was a pain no medicine could cure. She'd transferred from the A&E department to the Children's Ward in January, hoping that removing herself from

Gus's presence would be the first step in the healing process. It hadn't worked. Now it was June, and she still couldn't get him, what he'd done, or the barrage of conflicting emotions out of her mind. Even reading his name or seeing his handwriting twisted the knife that pierced her heart. And it hurt as much as ever.

Sensing she was being watched, Holly looked up and saw Sister Erica Sharpe's formidable form standing in the ward's office doorway. Erica beckoned her and Holly nodded her understanding. She hung the chart on the bed and ensured her young charge was comfortable before walking towards the office, wondering if they had a new admission to contend with. It had been a busy day, with several new patients coming in, and they had little space left for any more beds.

As Holly approached Erica remained in the doorway, hands planted on ample hips. She could be anywhere between fifty and seventy years of age—no one knew, and asking was out of the question. Erica had been part of the hospital since its transformation from a small cottage hospital to the well-equipped regional infirmary it had become, growing over the years in proportion with the way Strathlochan itself had expanded.

Erica had a fearsome reputation—Sharpe by name and, on occasion, sharp by nature—and even the most senior consultants had been known to quiver in their boots when on the receiving end of her displeasure. Student nurses approached her ward with awe and trepidation. Holly smiled, remembering her own scary first meeting with Erica. Several years on and she had huge respect for the woman who gave everything for her patients and under whose impressive bosom beat a heart of gold.

'Come in, Holly,' she invited, her sombre expression and the look in her eyes making Holly feel uneasy.

Inside the office Holly faltered, surprised to see Gina Adriani, one of her closest friends, sitting there. A fellow staff nurse, Gina had worked with her in A&E before leaving the previous summer to take up a position at Strathlochan's new multi-purpose drop-in centre. Just married and blissfully happy, today Gina looked uncharacteristically pensive and pale.

'Hello! What are you doing here? Have you

come to do some real work?' Holly joked, trying to shake off a sudden sense of foreboding.

'No, not that.'

Gina didn't return her smile and Holly's apprehension increased. 'What is it?'

'Sit down, my dear,' Erica advised, nudging a free chair closer to Gina's.

'What's going on?' Holly asked again, glad for the seat as her legs now felt too wobbly to hold her.

Erica never called anyone 'my dear' unless there was bad news. Holly's imagination ran wild and fear took hold. Had something happened to Seb, Gina's husband? Or to their mutual friends Rico and Ruth?

Before she could voice her anxiety Gina took her hand. 'I wish there was some better way to tell you.'

'Tell me what?' Holly's chest tightened as alarm increased. 'Gina?'

Her friend sucked in a breath. 'There's been a terrible road accident. Holly, it's Julia. She's been fatally injured.'

Holly reeled, suddenly feeling as if she was

dreaming. She groped for words, which at first would not come.

'Wh-What about the baby?' She somehow forced the question past the fear and shock that clogged her throat. 'It's not due until next month.'

'Julia was brought in by air ambulance and is in Theatre now. A specialist team is doing everything possible to save the baby,' Gina explained, but the words failed to quell the terror building within.

'Oh, my God.'

Holly sagged in the chair, her fingers tightening reflexively on Gina's as Erica rested an arm around her shoulders. Both women were talking, but Holly didn't hear a word: her heart was racing, every manic beat reverberating in her ears. As the horrific news sank in a range of mixed emotions and unanswered questions chased themselves through her head, and a cry of distress welled within her as she zeroed in on one thing.

One *person*.

Whatever else had happened, however much he'd hurt her, and however badly things had gone wrong, there was only one person she could think of now and only one place she needed to be.

'Gus,' she whispered, her voice raw with the pain searing through her. 'I have to go to him.'

CHAPTER TWO

HOLLY didn't care whether hospital rules discouraged running in the corridors. The only thought pounding in her mind as she raced out of the Children's Ward was to reach Gus as soon as possible.

'I don't know how the accident happened,' Gina said, keeping pace beside her. 'We had a phone call asking us to come in and give what support we could. I came to you…Seb went to find Gus.'

'Thank you.'

However conflicted her feelings, however strong the sense of betrayal, and however angry, hurt and upset she was with him, she couldn't bear the thought of Gus's grief. It was a relief to know Seb was with him. On the darkest and worst of days, when part of her had wanted to lash out at Gus, to hurt him as much as he'd hurt her, she would never have wished something this awful to happen.

Rather than wait for the lift Holly pushed open the door to the staff stairway, footsteps echoing as they hurried down two flights to the floor below. As they emerged into the wide corridor and approached the double doors of the operating suite their pace slowed and Gina rested a hand at the small of her back.

'Holly, I'm worried about you.'

'Worry about Gus and the baby,' she requested, her voice shaky. 'Not me.'

'I know how you feel, hon, but...'

As the anxious words trailed off Holly acknowledged that, although her best friend had some understanding of the situation, no one—not even Gina—knew the true extent of her feelings, because she'd worked so hard for so many months to hide them. She had presented an outward image of calm serenity to the world...one that belied the terrible pain, loss and the sense of betrayal that ripped her to shreds.

Before Gina could utter another word Holly opened the door and headed towards the waiting area. There were several people inside—Seb, a theatre representative, Frazer and Rick from the air ambulance, a policeman…and Gus. It was to the latter that her gaze was instinctively drawn.

Dressed in A&E scrubs, he stood apart from the others and a little ache settled inside her at how symbolic that was, how characteristic of the man she had come to know. A man who had been so alone and who found it so hard to let anyone get close to him. She'd breached that reserve and for a brief while had found the man within. And had fallen in love with him. Before everything had gone so spectacularly wrong.

She hadn't set eyes on Gus for weeks: a deliberate ploy but an unsuccessful one, because she hadn't stopped thinking about him for a moment. Anger and humiliation churned inside her, as did the fire of resentment and jealousy, and the hurt that never went away. She'd tried to convince herself she hated him—she certainly hated what he'd *done*—but she despaired of the part of herself that missed him and cared about him. Now, like someone parched with thirst stumbling on a fresh oasis, she greedily drank in the sight of him.

An inch or two under six feet, he wasn't the tallest man in the room, but to her he was the most impressive, the one who immediately held her attention. Even in the unflattering scrubs he looked heart-stoppingly handsome and intensely masculine. His thick dark brown hair was mussed—a result, she knew, of his characteristic habit of running a hand through it when he was stressed—and the way a few defiant strands flopped rakishly across his forehead was so familiar and endearing it brought a sting to her heart.

Her first instinct was to rush to him and hug him, needing both to comfort and be comforted, but as if he sensed her presence he turned to look at her. One glimpse at the stony mask on his unusually pale face and the distant expression in his smoky green eyes halted her in her tracks. Instinctively she shrank back.

That he was ravaged by shock was evident. But his pain also pained *her*, because it drove home again the way he'd publicly rejected her and chosen Julia…and how the two people she should have been able to trust most had hurt and betrayed her, leaving her the broken-hearted object of hospital gossip. Withdrawing into herself, she had wrestled with the stark contradiction and confusion. She remained filled with pain and bitter regret, yet a part of her couldn't stop caring about him.

Instinctively she clung to Gina's hand, allowing her friend to guide her to some nearby chairs to sit down. The tension in the room was palpable, and Holly tried to put her own feelings aside and assess what was happening. Frazer and Rick were in conversation with the policeman, giving their accounts, she assumed, of events at the scene of the accident. As for Gus, he was now talking with the woman from the operating room, and as Holly listened it became clear that his request to access Theatre had been refused. Moved to protest on his behalf, Holly stood up again, her legs trembling as she took a step forward to voice her own opinion.

'Surely Gus has a right to be in there?' she argued, all too conscious that the man in question was looking at her once more.

Gus stared at Holly in surprise. He hadn't expected such staunch support from her, but here she was, planting herself firmly in his corner, and there was no doubt her indignation was genuine.

'This is a difficult situation for both of you,' the theatre administrator responded, calm and yet firm, looking from Holly to Gus. 'But I'd ask for your patience. The specialist team are doing all they can to ensure the baby's survival. As soon as they are free to talk to you, one of the consultants will give you all the information you need.'

He hated being denied the opportunity to witness the moment his child came into the world, especially given the risk to his or her life, yet he understood from a medical perspective why they were keeping him out of the operating room.

'The most crucial thing is the baby,' he allowed, his voice hoarse, a mix of emotions raging inside him.

Holly nodded, and she was close enough that he heard the little hitch in her breath. 'I agree.'

As the theatre assistant left, and Holly returned to her seat next to Gina, Gus turned and gazed out of the window. The hospital sat on the side of a hill, and from here he could look over the valley in which the picturesque town of Strathlochan sprawled around two sides of the loch that gave it its name. The town drew patronage from a wide area, and many villages and isolated communities depended on Strathlochan's small but comprehensive services.

There had been times in the last few months when he'd wished he'd never set foot in Strathlochan, Gus admitted, running the fingers of one hand through his hair. Times when bitter regret and intense loneliness had overtaken the brief spell of unusual happiness he'd experienced when he'd first arrived, before things with Holly had turned sour.

Right now he was struggling to come to terms with the shock of hearing Robert speak the accident victim's name. The reality that Julia had been fatally injured brought feelings he couldn't allow himself to dwell on, because overshadowing everything was the knowledge that his baby's life hung in the balance.

It felt like hours, not minutes, since the helicopter had arrived and his world had turned upside down. He'd rushed up to the operating suite from A&E alone, the tension, fear and uncertainty of the wait making him nauseous. He had questions—many questions. Talking with Frazer and Rick was a priority, but they were still being questioned by one of the policemen investigating the accident.

An accident he couldn't understand.

Why had Julia been driving? As far as he knew she'd never had a licence. He'd parked his car in the hospital car park that morning, so how and when had she taken it? Where had she been? Why? And what had happened? The police would want answers, too, but they would have to wait— one issue overrode everything else.

Had his child won the battle for life?

A ragged breath shuddered through him and he tried to refocus his thoughts before they overwhelmed him.

Thoughts that slid inexorably back to Holly.

Seb Adriani had reached the operating suite's waiting area a few seconds after him. Gus didn't know the Italian doctor well—although he was the husband of one of Holly's best friends—but he'd been grateful when Seb had told him that Gina was with Holly. At least he'd had some forewarning of her possible arrival.

But nothing had prepared him for the moment when she'd walked into the waiting room. After weeks, months, of not seeing her, the instant he'd been aware of her presence and turned to look at her he'd experienced a whole gamut of confusing emotions. The first thing he'd wanted to do in these most desperate of circumstances was to take her in his arms and hold her, but as she'd hesitated and turned away from him he'd managed to prevent himself from doing anything stupid. He'd made a fool of himself over Holly once. He didn't plan on doing it again.

On edge and impatient, Gus wrestled with his reaction to Holly. He could see her now, her image reflected in the glass of the window as she sat across the room, and he shifted to bring her more into focus. In her smart, staff-nurse's uniform, and with her shoulder-length wavy blonde hair tied back in a short ponytail, she looked fresh-faced, incredibly young...and scared.

Her flawless skin was ashen, so pale that the cute smattering of freckles dusting her cheek-bones and the bridge of her nose were more noticeable than usual, while her sky-blue eyes, fringed by long sooty lashes, looked far too big and bruised with worry. Drawn to her, he turned around, his disobedient gaze clashing with hers. Tension hummed between them for several long moments. He tried to look away but found he couldn't, held as if by some invisible force.

It was the sudden arrival of one of the consultants that ended the strange and uncomfortable interlude.

'Gus Buchanan and Holly Tait?' the man queried, pushing through the heavy swing door into the room, the mask he had worn in Theatre now hanging limply around his neck. 'You're the relatives?'

'Yes,' Gus confirmed, stepping forward as Holly stood up. He recognised the man by sight, and knew of his reputation, but they'd never met before.

'I'm Shaun Haggerty, consultant neonatologist.' The introductions made, he shook hands with them both. 'If you come with me, I'll bring you up to speed on what's happened and we can discuss in private what you want to do.'

Intensely aware of Holly's presence, Gus held open the door of the waiting room, finding it hard to breathe past the restriction in his throat, scared at what he was about to hear regarding the condition of his baby.

* * *

'Seb and I will wait here in case you need us,' Gina promised, and Holly nodded her appreciation before she forced unsteady legs to move.

She followed Gus and Mr Haggerty down the hall and into a small nondescript office. Her stomach was so churned up with emotion that she felt positively ill, and she couldn't stop shaking. As Mr Haggerty closed the door and walked around the desk Holly sat on the vacant chair next to Gus.

'This has been a big shock for you both,' Mr Haggerty began, his expression sombre. 'I'm sure you have a lot of questions. The police are investigating the accident and will want to talk to you, so I'll leave that side of things to them and deal only with the medical issues.' He paused, looking from Gus to her and back again. 'Is that all right with you?'

'Yes. Thank you. Right now I just want to know about the baby,' Gus replied, and tears stung Holly's eyes at the unmistakable desperation in his voice—a desperation that matched her own.

Realising both men were waiting for her response, Holly nodded her agreement, too off-balance for more coherent thought. 'Me, too.'

As she spoke she was painfully conscious that none of them had mentioned Julia. She glanced at Gus. His face was a mask, revealing none of the emotion she knew must be rampaging through him. Instinctively she wanted to comfort him, and to seek comfort in return, but the special rapport they'd once shared had broken down so completely she was now nervous and uncertain of his reaction. So she curbed the urge to reach for his hand, and as the consultant began speaking she focused on his words.

'I'm afraid Mrs Buchanan suffered serious head, neck and facial injuries,' Mr Haggerty informed them, and Holly closed her eyes at the horror that had befallen her sister. 'The air ambulance was returning from transferring a patient to Glasgow when the call came in to attend the car crash, which meant they were close by and on scene within minutes,' he continued, leaning forward and steepling his fingers together. 'The flight doctor and the paramedic detected a weak foetal heartbeat and did everything they could to maintain the baby's life in order to reach the hospital.'

Holly flicked another quick glance towards Gus

in time to see him running fingers through his hair—such a familiar sign of his stress and agitation.

'The only blessing to emerge from this tragedy is thanks to Frazer and Rick,' the consultant added, the ghost of a smile relieving the sternness of his expression.

'How do you mean?' Gus asked, his voice hoarse.

Holly clenched her hands together until the knuckles turned white, hoping and praying that there was still hope for the baby.

'There is much we still need to talk about,' Mr Haggerty stressed, 'but I can tell you, Gus, that thanks to the quick actions of the flight crew, combined with the skill and determination of everyone in Theatre, you now have a son.'

A son.

He had a *son*.

The words hammered inside Gus's head, and for several moments all he could hear was the rushing of blood in his veins as it pulsed with a matching rhythm…a son, a son, a son, a son.

A shiver of reaction ran down his spine. As he

struggled to control the welling of emotion that brought an uncharacteristic sting to his eyes he felt the light brush of Holly's fingers on the back of his hand. Without conscious thought he gratefully accepted the physical contact, moving so they were palm to palm, their fingers naturally interlocking.

'My s-son…?' he asked, stumbling as he voiced the word aloud for the first time. 'How is he?'

'He's a fighter. Given the trauma of the accident and the delivery—and the suggestion that he could be up to four weeks premature—he's in miraculously good shape. So far,' Mr Haggerty informed them.

Relieved despite the words of caution, Gus expelled a shaky breath. 'Thank God.'

Holly's fingers tightened on his and he returned the pressure, overwhelmed after the nerve-racking and stressful wait for news that his son was alive. Not only alive, but by all accounts with a real chance of survival.

'We're transferring him to the paediatric intensive care unit in the maternity wing so we can monitor him closely,' the consultant continued. 'He's small. And he's bruised. It appears your wife wasn't wearing her seatbelt, so he must have taken a battering in the crash, and then there was his somewhat unceremonious entry into the world. We need to do some tests—'

'What kind of tests?' Gus demanded, anxiety once more rising within him.

'As I said, your son seems remarkably robust. At the moment we can't tell whether he's suffered any ill-effects from the accident…how long he experienced any loss of oxygen or blood-flow, for example. There are a couple of other issues we need to clarify with you, too,' the man added, a frown on his face.

Gus's chest tightened. 'What kind of issues? What's wrong?'

'We have questions about the validity of his due date—'

'There's no doubt about that,' Gus interrupted, tension ripping through him. It was one of the few things he *was* certain about.

The older man raised an eyebrow. 'No room for error at all?' he asked, a note of disbelief edging his voice.

'None,' Gus confirmed, although he had no intention of explaining *why* he was so certain about his baby's conception—especially in front of Holly.

'If that's so,' the consultant remarked, his doubts obvious, 'then he's unusually well-developed. He's not displaying the signs of prematurity we would expect in a baby of that age.'

'Maybe the upheaval of the accident and delivery are masking other things,' Holly suggested softly.

Gus glanced at her, noting the pallor of her skin and feeling the tremor of her hand in his. Her support of him took his breath away. And confused him. Guilt and self-disgust about the fateful night in question—the one that had resulted in the baby and sparked off everything else—returned with a vengeance. As did the memory of Holly's reaction…her anger, confusion, hurt, and the cool disdain in her eyes when she'd looked at him that had chilled him to the marrow of his bones.

A short-lived but virulent virus which had kept him off work for a few days had knocked him for six—as had the medication prescribed to combat some of the more debilitating symptoms. Only the prospect of his first proper date with Holly could have tempted him out that evening. A date which, he'd hoped, would mark a turning point in their relationship, moving it from platonic friendship to something more intimate and permanent.

He'd been waiting for Holly in the Strathlochan Arms, the favoured haunt of many of the local services personnel, where he'd been renting a room until contracts were signed and he could move into his new house. Holly had not only stood him up without contacting him herself, but she'd ensured her rejection was delivered in the most public and humiliating of ways in front of many of their colleagues.

He'd been ridiculously early, sitting at a table near the log fire and counting the seconds until Holly's arrival, excitement and hopeful expectation firing his blood and distracting him from how rough he was feeling. A change in the atmosphere had drawn his attention and he'd glanced up to see a striking-looking woman walking towards him. A noticeable buzz of tension and anticipation had rippled through those present in the bar.

There had been no doubting the stranger's outward beauty, capturing as she had the interest of most of the men in the room—and the envy of many of the women. She'd been tall, her platinum-blonde hair sleek and styled to perfection, its fashionable cut framing the somewhat angular bone structure of her face. Given the colour of her skin, she had been no stranger to sun-beds and fake tan. Her hazel eyes had been almond-shaped, her nose narrow and up-tilted at the tip, while her pouting lips—which he'd suspected were a result of filler injections rather than Mother Nature—had been defined with siren-red lipstick. Skin-tight jeans tucked inside knee-length leather boots had emphasised long, long legs, while an expensive cashmere top had clung to her slender figure.

In Gus's view she had been too slender, too polished and too artificial. He'd infinitely preferred Holly's womanly curves and natural beauty. The disinterested assessment had run rapidly through his mind as the unknown woman approached him, and he'd regarded her with suspicion when she stopped at his table.

'Are you Gus Buchanan?' she asked, her head tilted coquettishly to one side.

Wary, Gus nodded. 'Yes, I am. Why?'

'My name is Julia Tait.' The woman paused for a moment before completing her introduction. 'I'm Holly's sister.'

'Her *sister*?' Gus repeated, aware of the shock and confusion in his voice.

'Let me guess… Holly never told you about me.'

Embarrassed by the unexpected situation, Gus frowned, puzzled and annoyed by Holly's blatant omission—and Julia's apparent expectation of it. 'No. No, I—'

'Don't worry, I'm used to it,' Julia admitted, rescuing him from his clumsy efforts to explain the unexplainable. With a sigh, she shook her head. 'I'm afraid Holly has been lost to me for some time…she only acknowledges me or asks for help when she wants something. And this time, I'm afraid, my uncomfortable mission is to tell you that Holly's changed her mind about dating you. She's not coming, Gus…tonight or any other night.'

As she paused something flashed in her eyes, but it was gone before he could identify it. He was having enough trouble hiding his dismay as the full realisation of what she was saying sank in.

'I'm really sorry, Gus, but Holly doesn't want to go out with you.'

CHAPTER THREE

'I SEE.' Gus had struggled to mask his bitter disappointment, hurt and confusion. 'Why can't Holly tell me herself?'

Julia had sighed, shaking her head. 'That's Holly for you. She gets in too deep and expects someone else—me—to do her dirty work.'

Irritation rose within him—not just because Holly had stood him up but because she had chosen not to do the decent thing and say so herself. Not to mention the fact that she had kept things from him…like the existence of a sister. Given that he'd opened up to her about his past as he'd never done with anyone else before, with Holly professing her understanding about why family was so important to him, it was even stranger that she'd declined to tell him the truth about her own. It seemed out of character for the Holly he knew. But maybe he didn't know her after all. Wary and cautious, he'd begun re-establishing his protective guard, afraid his fledgling trust had been misplaced.

'May I sit down?'

Julia's query had cut through his thoughts. He'd wanted to say no, to be left alone so he could retreat to his room to think over Holly's rejection—a rejection witnessed by colleagues present in the bar.

Sensing that he and Julia were being watched, Gus reluctantly succumbed to politeness. 'Of course,' he invited, waiting as she pulled up a chair and sat down opposite him before good manners drove him to prolong the awkward and unwanted encounter. 'Would you like a drink?'

A smile curved her mouth. 'Thanks. A vodka and orange, please.'

Gus rose to his feet, pausing with one hand resting on the table as light-headedness assailed him. He made his way to the bar, conscious of people looking at him, and along with Julia's drink he was grateful for the glass of iced water the landlady gave him.

'Still feeling rotten, Gus?' the kindly woman asked him.

He nodded in assent, regretting it immediately

when the headache hammering inside his skull intensified. 'Unfortunately, yes,' he admitted, managing a smile.

As he made his way back to his table Gus noticed Julia bending forward, apparently engrossed with something he couldn't see. Before he could rejoin her he was waylaid by one of his colleagues, who was pulling on his coat and on the point of leaving.

'Gus?' Dr Trevor Wilkinson—a registrar, Strathlochan born and bred, who had recently returned to work in A&E following a long spell of illness—rested a hand on Gus' arm, detaining him. 'You don't look well. The medication not helping?'

'The pills have improved things. I just react badly to them,' Gus admitted wryly, understanding for the first time why some patients complained that the side-effects of the medication they were prescribed were as bad as, or worse than, the condition with which they'd been diagnosed.

Trevor gestured to the glasses Gus was carrying. 'You'd do better taking it easy on the alcohol, then!'

'Mine's water—I don't drink.'

'Good. You'll need all your wits about you,' the registrar advised cryptically.

Gus frowned. 'How do you mean?'

'You're playing with fire,' Trevor replied, lowering his voice so those nearby couldn't hear. 'I hope you know what you're doing, Gus.'

The comments puzzled him, but Trevor was gone, edging through the crowd, before Gus could question him further.

Perplexed by the conversation, Gus returned to his table. Julia, still with her back to him, glanced round briefly, before making a couple of furtive movements out of his sight, but by the time he sat down and met her gaze she was smiling at him, the picture of innocence.

'Thank you for this,' she said, taking a sip of her drink.

Gus nodded, still nonplussed and knocked off-kilter by the events of the evening. Feeling too warm, he shifted along the banquette away from the heat of the log fire, his hand coming into contact with his mobile phone as he did so. He'd had no idea it had slipped from his pocket. Surreptitiously he checked the screen, but there were no tell-tale indications of missed calls or texts. What had he expected? That Julia was wrong and Holly had tried to contact him? Disenchanted, his hopes dashed, he refocused his attention on the unwanted companion opposite him.

'What happened between you and Holly?' he forced himself to ask, taking a long drink of ice-cold water.

Julia looked sad, but resigned, and the story she told him of her estrangement from her younger sister touched his heart, resonating as it did with his own lack of family. And he couldn't help but be further disappointed in Holly. Not only had she listened to his explanation about his background but she'd professed her sorrow and understanding. She had even cried for him.

Had they been crocodile tears? It appeared so. If Holly *had* understood, surely she would have told him about Julia. In one night the only woman he'd ever believed himself in love with had rejected him publicly in front of their colleagues, and he had discovered she had also lied to him by omission. What else didn't he know about her?

Hurt, upset and confused, he drained his glass

before leaning back and closing his eyes. His head was pounding. The virus and the pills were still affecting him, leaving him feeling hot and cold at the same time, his whole body aching, and occasional waves of nausea gripping his stomach.

'Are you all right?' Julia asked with concern.

'I'm sorry.' He might be a loner, and unused to socialising, but he disliked rudeness, and guilt assailed him for his lack of manners. Gus gave himself a mental shake. 'I've not been feeling too good.'

Julia rose elegantly to her feet and picked up his empty glass. 'Let me get you another drink. Unless you'd rather have a coffee or something to eat?'

'No!' His negative response was swift, the very thought of coffee and food causing his stomach to rebel once more. 'Just water. Thanks.'

Julia soon returned, this time choosing to sit next to him on the banquette. Disconcerted, Gus nevertheless welcomed the glass of water she handed him, which this time had twists of lemon and lime in it.

'Thanks,' he murmured, taking a long drink. It tasted a bit odd, but he was thirsty enough to ignore it—although he did set the citrus slices aside.

'If it's any consolation, Gus, it isn't you. Holly's shy of commitment. This is by no means the first time that she's led a man on and given him false hope,' Julia informed him sadly, the scarlet-tipped fingers of one hand coming to rest on his jean-clad thigh. 'I think it stems from her engagement all those years ago.'

Diverting his attention from her unwanted touch, Julia's latest revelation delivered another hammer blow. Gus reeled, turning to Julia in shock.

'Holly was very young—still a teenager,' she continued, looking into his eyes, her own gleaming large and wistful. 'She and Euan were childhood sweethearts—Euan was besotted with her. At the eleventh hour Holly dumped him. Aside from the embarrassment of cancelling arrangements, returning presents and explaining to everyone, Euan was devastated.' She paused a moment, her expression sombre. 'There was no reasoning with Holly. She refused to talk with Euan again. Since then she's done what she's doing with you...allowed men to get close, only to back off when they want to take things further.'

The engagement was another thing Holly had failed to tell him about. Why? If he was to believe her sister, it was all Holly's fault. He didn't want it to be true…it was contrary to all he had thought Holly to be. But after this evening he couldn't help but wonder who Holly really was and if she'd fooled him completely.

Gus ran a hand through his hair in agitation, wishing his head would clear as he struggled to reconcile what Julia had told him with the Holly he had *thought* he knew. Feeling increasingly fuzzy-headed and out of sorts, he took another drink.

'Poor Gus,' Julia sympathised, leaning closer and resting her arm around his shoulder. 'This is the last thing you need when you're feeling so ill. Holly should be here, caring for you.'

'I'm OK,' he refuted, frowning in confusion as he heard himself slurring the words. What was wrong with him? He felt worse now than when the virus had been at its most virulent.

With a wry laugh, Julia gave him a hug. 'Sure you are.'

'I'm used to being alone.'

'Me, too,' Julia confided, all trace of humour gone. 'And that's so sad…for both of us.' She paused, head tilted to one side as she studied him. 'You should be in bed, Gus. Come on, I'll help you to your room.'

Finding it difficult to focus on anything, Gus felt too ill to argue. He craved the sanctuary of his room, and allowed Julia to assist him as he summoned his last reserves of energy and struggled to his feet, swaying alarmingly. Julia remained at his side, holding him steady, and he draped an arm around her to brace himself.

He vaguely remembered walking unsteadily out of the bar, but he had no recollection of the journey down the pub's corridor, nor the arrival at his room. Nor did he have any memories of what had happened next. Only that he'd woken in the morning with a thudding headache, horrified to find that not only was Julia real, and not a figment of his fevered imagination, but she was curled up next to him in bed…and both of them were naked.

Edging away from her, he'd flung an arm across his sore eyes and stifled a groan, a rush of confusion, guilt and self-disgust sweeping through him. The virus, pills and disappointment over Holly's rejection were not sufficient excuses for his behaviour. And he'd compounded that bad behaviour by pretending to be asleep when Julia stirred so he wouldn't have to face her. Thankfully she'd seemed as keen as he to avoid a post-mortem as she'd risen and swiftly dressed before quietly letting herself out of his room.

He hadn't wanted to talk with Julia, but that had been as nothing compared to his reluctance at the thought of seeing Holly—of not only dealing with what he had done, but confronting her about her rejection and the various things she had kept from him. A fresh wave of nausea had assailed him.

Illness had kept him in bed and away from work for another twenty-four hours. Had he known in advance how terrible his return to A&E and the scene with Holly were going to be, he might have stayed in bed for ever.

He'd certainly had no idea how horribly that wretched night would come back to haunt him, destroying his relationship with Holly and resulting in the announcement that Julia was expecting his child. An announcement that had led him into an unwanted, loveless marriage with only months to prepare for his unexpected role as a father.

It had terrified him

It still did, he acknowledged, reality slamming him back to the present. For now he had to push all the pain and emotion of the past from his mind and focus on the baby. *His* baby—for whom he had sacrificed himself and endured months of unhappiness.

With Julia.

Without Holly.

He listened as Shaun Haggerty responded to Holly's suggestion about the baby's prematurity. 'We will, of course, continue to observe him closely.'

'You said there was another problem?' Gus prompted, grateful they were moving on from the awkward issue of conception.

'Yes.' The consultant opened a file, glancing at something before looking up again, apology in his eyes. 'I don't like to press you on such things at this distressing time, but my concern is your son's health. So I need to ask…Was your wife drinking during her pregnancy?'

Gus sat back in shock, totally unprepared for the question. 'No! Absolutely not,' he refuted, a sick feeling in his stomach.

There was much about Julia he didn't know. There had been times when her mercurial temper and unpredictable mood swings had made life especially difficult. But surely he would have noticed something so far amiss?

'There's no alcohol in the house. I don't drink, and I never saw Julia drink after she knew she was expecting a child,' he continued, feeling the gentle squeeze of Holly's fingers. 'She found pregnancy difficult—she was quite ill. And she gave up smoking, too. She knew her health was important for the baby.'

Or so he'd thought.

Mr Haggerty nodded and wrote a note in the file, but his frown remained. 'I had to ask, Gus, I'm sorry. There was an almost empty bottle of gin in the car, and tests have revealed that Julia was more than three times over the drink-drive limit. We need to know if this was a one-off aberration or something that might have a longer-term effect on your baby. There's no evidence of foetal alcohol syndrome, but we're running tests to be on the safe side.'

Gus swore under his breath. He was stunned. And angry. Julia had relied on him to take her wherever she'd wanted to go, claiming she didn't drive, so he had no idea why and how she'd taken his car—or where she'd been. The news that she'd been irresponsible enough to drink excessively before getting behind the wheel astounded and infuriated him. It was bad enough that she'd brought about her own injuries, but to risk the life of others, including her unborn child, was unforgivable.

He met Holly's gaze and saw the dismay and concern in her sky-blue eyes. They both knew what long-term alcohol consumption could do to a growing baby, and he hoped with all his heart that Julia's rash behaviour that day *was* the aberration the consultant suggested and nothing worse. His son had enough to battle against without inherited alcohol problems on top.

Whatever else had occurred between them, and however hard things had been in recent months, he knew he'd been diligent in his care of both Julia and the baby. But he hadn't been there twenty-four hours a day. Nor had he been Julia's keeper. He'd trusted her to keep her side of the bargain…that she'd do all she could to protect herself and their unborn child. Now that trust had been broken in the worst possible way.

'I want to see my son,' he announced gruffly, releasing Holly's hand and rising impatiently to his feet.

'Of course. And you will…very soon,' the consultant placated him, gesturing back to the chair. 'If you can bear with me a little longer, Gus? I know this isn't easy for you, or for Holly, but I have to ask you about Julia.'

Unsettled, and overwhelmed by the myriad emotions fighting inside him, Gus reluctantly sat down again, feeling bereft without the comfort of Holly's hand in his. He was alarmed that he'd felt the once-familiar kick in the gut and tingle down the spine when he'd looked at her. He felt guilty for his response to Holly, and even guiltier for begrudging Mr Haggerty the time he wanted to spend talking about Julia. On a human level he felt deep shock and sadness for her, but the only thing driving him on was a desperation to see his son.

He met Holly's gaze, unable to read her thoughts. She was clearly deeply affected by events—her support had been genuine—but he was less able to gauge her feelings about her older sister. They'd not been close. He smothered a humourless laugh at the understatement. He understood little of the complex situation between the two women—a situation he'd been unwittingly drawn into.

Not that he was in any position to judge the level of Holly's grief for Julia. He felt the pressing weight of guilt and shame as he forced himself to admit the truth. That whilst he would never have wished this tragedy on Julia, the primary rush of emotion he'd experienced was not grief, as everyone assumed, but relief.

Relief at being freed from the loveless, lonely marriage they'd endured these last months… months when they'd played their roles well enough to convince those around them that their relationship was real.

Holly had no idea what Gus was thinking, but when she felt the full force of his smoky green gaze on her she was unable to prevent a quiver of reaction. Her hand still tingled from his touch. She'd been unable to resist the urge to reach out to him, driven by the emotion in his voice when he'd learned about his son. Fresh tears stung her eyes as she recalled the way he'd responded, taking her hand, linking their fingers and holding on tight, creating a shared bond between them… one that had seemed so natural months ago but which now left her confused and puzzled.

Gus looked away, releasing her from his magnetic hold. A ragged breath whispered from her. Without the comfort of holding his hand she felt bereft and alone. The shock of all that had happened was taking its toll, and the tension between Gus and herself made everything more difficult. She was still angry at the way he'd so publicly rejected her and made her the centre of gossip. The pain and betrayal at the knowledge of Julia's pregnancy had never lessened. Now the baby was here, having survived a traumatic birth, and she was swamped by a rush of conflicting emotions.

After months of attempting to put distance between them, the last thing she wanted was to spend time with Gus again, and yet her first instinct on learning of the tragedy had been to run to him. Clasping her shaking hands together, Holly glanced at Gus. They'd been united by events and a shared concern for the baby, and somehow she had to find a way of putting her jumbled feelings about Gus aside.

Gus remained silent and remote, so Holly forced herself to ask the question that was hanging in the air. 'Wh-What about Julia?'

Mr Haggerty sighed and shook his head. 'There's no hope for her, I'm afraid. As I explained, her injuries were so severe that, had it not been for signs of life from the baby, she would have been declared dead at the scene of the accident. In order to save the baby and maintain his oxygen and blood-flow, she was placed on life support. We'd like your permission to turn that off. But first there's the delicate issue of asking you to consider the possibility of organ donation. I appreciate how difficult it is, but you know time is critical. My advice, for what it's worth, is to look to the future…to the miracle of this baby,' the older man finished with sympathy.

'Holly, what do you want to do?' Gus asked gruffly, taking her by surprise by including her. 'Did Julia express her views to you on donating?'

'I know she didn't carry a donor card, but we never discussed it. Personally I'm fully in favour of giving someone on the transplant waiting list the chance of a better life, but I'll support whatever decision you make,' she told him, conscious that helping others had never been a high priority for her sister.

'Like Holly, I support the donor programme. Let's hope that along with the baby some good can come from this tragedy.' A silence stretched heavily for a long moment before Gus continued, his voice raw. 'I think we should take medical advice and let Julia rest in peace.'

Holly was relieved they were on the same wavelength—on this, at least. 'I agree. It's the right thing to do, Gus.'

'I know it isn't an easy decision, but I hope the knowledge that other people's lives will be saved might help a little,' Mr Haggerty offered, scribbling notes in the file. 'And I can assure you Julia will be treated with every care and respect.'

'Thank you.' Gus's tone was stiff and guarded. 'Will there need to be an official identification?'

Holly sucked in a breath. This was something she hadn't thought about. She glanced at Gus but could read none of his emotions. What must this be doing to him? And how could he bear it if he had to identify Julia? There and then she decided that if he was called on to perform the task he would not be doing it alone. It was the last thing she wanted, but she would be there for him—even though his pain and grief over Julia twisted the knife ever more cruelly inside her.

'As I said, the police will be speaking with you and helping you through the aftermath of this dreadful event. There'll be a routine investigation, and you'll be kept informed of the outcome,' the consultant told them, rolling his pen in his fingers. 'But you won't be asked to identify her. The police are satisfied with the chain of evidence…and I'm sad to say the accident has rendered her facially unrecognisable.'

Although relieved that she and Gus would be spared one trauma, Holly wrestled with the disturbing reality of Julia's injuries. What a tragic irony that in death her sister had lost the thing she'd most valued in life—her looks. She couldn't bear to think of the horror Julia had experienced, or how much she might have known and suffered. However bad their relationship, however much

Julia had hurt her, and however much she'd hated her sister's betrayals—most recently and painfully with Gus—she would never have wished such a devastating accident on her.

'Does Julia have any unique distinguishing marks?'

Mr Haggerty's question drew Holly from her thoughts. To her surprise Gus remained silent, his gaze averted, and realising he must be in shock, and had no intention of answering, she spoke up. 'There's her tattoo.'

'A tattoo? Can you describe it?' the consultant asked, raising one thick dark eyebrow.

'Julia had it done at sixteen as an act of rebellion,' Holly explained. A shiver ran through her as she recalled the uproar her sister had joyfully provoked over the tattoo. 'There were big rows—especially with our father. It's of a mouth—scarlet lips, shaped as if blowing a kiss—and there are words around it.'

'What words? And where is the tattoo?' Mr Haggerty queried, making notes.

A soft bloom of colour pinkened her cheeks. 'It's on her right buttock, and the words read

"Kiss my butt",' she admitted with a nervous laugh, her blush deepening.

'Very distinctive,' Mr Haggerty replied, with a small smile of his own.

The brief moment of unexpected and embarrassed humour failed to lessen the tension that hung in the room, and Holly felt increasingly conscious of Gus's brooding presence. Gus, who had hurt her so badly and who, despite everything, she could not abandon, even though his grief for her sister and the reality of their baby only magnified her own pain.

Holly jumped as the shrill sound of a pager broke the silence.

'That's mine,' Mr Haggerty confirmed. 'Excuse me a moment.'

As he reached for the phone on the desk and made a quick call Holly met Gus's gaze, her heart squeezing at the distant, withdrawn look in his gorgeous green eyes. The chasm between them seemed more intimidating than ever. The days ahead would be difficult, and with no idea what the future held in store she felt anxious and uncertain.

'There'll be other questions, I'm sure, but I

think we've covered all we need to for now,' the consultant said softly, putting down the phone and closing the file. 'That was my registrar calling from PICU. They've finished the current tests and the baby is now settled and stable.'

'Thank God.'

Gus's heartfelt words and the shimmer of moisture in his eyes made Holly's chest tighten. Her voice wavered as she asked the question she knew Gus wanted answered as urgently as she did. 'Can we see him now?'

'Of course,' Mr Haggerty allowed, standing up and rounding the desk.

As Gus rose swiftly to his feet Holly followed suit, disconcerted by the frown he shot towards her. What was he thinking? Was he cross about the moment of laughter over Julia's tattoo? Or didn't he want her to see the baby? Filled with stubborn determination, she raised her chin in challenge. However difficult it proved to be, and however much it deepened her own pain and sense of emptiness, no one—not even Gus— would keep her from her nephew.

After offering his condolences and his continuing support, Mr Haggerty shook their hands.

Then, smiling broadly for the first time, he opened the door and issued the longed-for invitation.

'Gus, it's time for you to meet your son.'

CHAPTER FOUR

'HE IS *so* beautiful.'

Gus couldn't help the ghost of a smile that formed at the awed reverence in Holly's softly spoken words—words she had repeated countless times since they'd entered the Paediatric Intensive Care Unit and met his son.

His son.

He would never forget the moment he'd looked at and held his child for the first time. He'd thought his heart would burst right out of his chest, and his eyes had stung with uncharacteristic tears. That the baby was stable and robust enough to be picked up had been a joyful surprise. At first he'd been terrified of hurting or dropping him, his hands seeming too large and clumsy, but he'd soon adjusted and had felt the same kind of awe and amazement Holly had expressed.

He'd also experienced an immediate welling of

love. It had never happened to him before and, given his background, he'd never expected it to. He was accustomed to being alone, so when he'd come to Strathlochan the previous August and had met Holly he'd been shocked by his feelings for her and the way he'd been able to talk to her. He'd opened up to her as he never had with anyone else and, for a time, he'd dared to believe their instinctive friendship would lead to something more intimate and permanent.

But he'd been wrong.

So wrong.

He wished he could blame Holly for everything, but whilst it was true she'd lied to him, kept things from him and rejected him, he was solely responsible for his actions from the moment Julia had walked up to his table.

Ruthlessly, desperately, he slammed the door of his mind shut as the memories of that night and what had followed threatened to overwhelm him. There would be time to rake over the past, but his focus now was on his son—the prize who made everything worthwhile.

After the night of Holly's humiliating rejection and his own stupid mistakes he'd retreated back into himself, not anticipating ever being vulnerable to or caring about anyone again. Once more he'd been wrong. His heart had opened wide the instant he'd seen his child and he knew he'd do everything to protect, guard and love his unplanned but oh, so precious son.

None of his medical training had prepared him for seeing his own fragile baby connected up to IV lines and monitors. The tiny body had been pale and bruised after the trauma of the accident and an emergency Caesarean, but his heart-rate had settled and he was breathing on his own: excellent signs given the stress he'd been under. Julia had haemorrhaged so badly that the baby had, indeed, needed the blood transfusion Robert Mowbray had predicted.

In these early stages two unanswered questions rose above the others. Had the baby been starved of oxygen or blood supply long enough to cause brain or organ damage? And had he been adversely affected by Julia's consumption of alcohol? It would be a while before they knew, and Gus had never felt so scared or so helpless.

The ordeal would have been worse had he been living through it alone—his default position. But he wasn't on his own: despite all that had gone wrong between them Holly had remained staunch in her support of him and her concern for his son. He had no idea *why* Holly was doing what she was doing. It didn't make sense. She'd made it clear there was no room in her life for him, and she'd shown no interest whatsoever in her sister's pregnancy.

There had been no rows, no raised voices… He would have found it easier had Holly reacted that way. Instead she'd remained frighteningly cool, exuding a calm dignity that had made him feel worse than ever. But what had cut him to the core had been the disappointment, regret and disdain in her eyes when she'd looked at him. Now, after months of silence, Holly was reacting in a way he hadn't anticipated, and part of him remained reserved and aloof, confused by Holly and how she made him feel.

But, however much she puzzled him, he was grateful for Holly's support. She had already eased one embarrassing moment, coming to the rescue when Mr Haggerty had asked about Julia's distinguishing marks. He hadn't relished admitting zero knowledge of Julia's tattoo. Doing so would have meant revealing that he'd never seen his own wife naked. Gus bit back a mirthless laugh as he imagined the unwanted speculation *that* information would spark.

He looked at Holly, sitting on a chair beside the special cot. There was a soft, loving expression on her face as she gazed at the sleeping infant, but a shadow of pain remained in her eyes, arousing his curiosity. Something twisted inside him… something scary and unsettling. Alarmed, he dragged his gaze away, relieved when he looked towards the doorway and saw Seb and Gina approaching them. The couple had been unobtrusive but supportive, and Gus was grateful.

Gina rested a hand on Holly's shoulder, and Holly glanced up at her friend with a tired smile. 'Hi.'

'I've brought your bag and things from your locker,' Gina said, handing them over before she turned, including Gus in her smile. 'If there's nothing else you need, we're going to head home and give you some space.'

He watched as Holly swivelled on the chair and gave her friend and Seb a hug. 'Thank you both—for everything.'

'You've been great, thanks,' Gus echoed sincerely.

'We haven't done much.' Gina grimaced. 'I'm just so sorry. We're here any time at all if you need us.'

Seb nodded his agreement. 'Please ring, either of you, if there is anything we can do, or if you want to talk.'

Gus couldn't imagine doing so—asking for help was alien to him—but he appreciated the offer, surprised by how open and friendly Seb and Gina had been with him. He shook hands with the handsome Italian doctor, and was further taken aback when Gina gave him a hug, too.

As the couple left after a final round of goodbyes he noticed the way Holly watched them, as if she wanted to go with them rather than remain with him. The knowledge stung and increased his defensiveness.

'If there's somewhere else you'd rather be you don't have to stay,' he remarked, a sharper edge to his voice than he'd intended.

Holly didn't look at him, but he saw her shoulders stiffen. 'There's nothing more important than the baby.'

'You didn't show any interest during Julia's pregnancy,' Gus pointed out, confusion and hurt driving the accusation. 'You never once came to the house.'

'I was never once invited. And I didn't think I'd be welcome.'

Holly's words and the soft, sad tone in which she voiced them gave him pause. He wanted to continue to blame her—it made it much easier to maintain a distance that way—but…

'Julia said she approached you when she discovered she was pregnant and you turned her away.' As he forced out the words he saw the genuine surprise and puzzlement in her response.

'That's not true.' She shook her head, a few honey-blonde strands escaping her ponytail and feathering her pale face. Sky-blue eyes, clear and direct, gazed into his. 'Julia would never have come to me. Our relationship broke down years ago. She always knew how to hurt me most… and this time she excelled herself.'

Gus didn't know why, but he believed her—although he had no idea what lay behind her final words. Nor did he know why the sisters had become estranged. Hell, he hadn't even known

Holly *had* a sister until that fateful night at the Strathlochan Arms, when his life had changed for ever. It was one of the questions that remained unanswered: why, when they had been so close, and he'd thought so honest with each other, had Holly withheld the information about her sister and former fiancé? Especially once she'd known what the idea of family meant to him.

Before he could say more one of the specialist nurses monitoring the baby's condition came to carry out scheduled observations. Holly stood up to give the woman room.

'If you'll excuse me? I'm going to freshen up.'

Picking up her bag, she headed towards the restroom. Her chin was raised in stubborn but dignified defiance, and although she appeared outwardly calm he had seen the hurt in her eyes. He hurt, too. He just didn't know what or who to believe any more. Could he come to trust Holly again? Or had too much happened for them ever to re-establish any kind of friendship?

Holly had let him down. The disappointment and pain of her rejection and lies persisted. Yet he couldn't deny responsibility for his own part in events. Guilt and self-disgust weighed heavily upon him. Having avoided each other for months, Gus was sure the last thing either of them wanted was to be thrown together by the tragedy of Julia's death and the survival of the baby.

And for now he needed to maintain his guard— because he feared he remained as vulnerable to Holly as ever.

Thankful for the time alone, Holly sucked in a steadying breath and cast a quick look at her reflection in the restroom mirror. There was more colour in her cheeks. Now she had to return to the unit, when what she really wanted was to sneak home and lick her wounds. Wounds she had tried to convince herself were healing but which were, as these last hours had proved, quite evidently as raw and painful as ever.

But she couldn't leave. This was no longer about her and Gus. Now it was about the baby. A baby who tore at her heart and made the empty void inside her ache anew, but with whom she had fallen in love the moment she'd seen him, held him and breathed in his unique baby scent. She wanted to be involved in her nephew's life, although it would mean a level of involvement with Gus that she didn't know how to cope with.

However much she might want to, she couldn't forget that Gus was grieving for the wife he'd just lost: her sister. The woman he had chosen instead of *her*. A blatant, public betrayal by both Gus and Julia that hurt as much now as it had then. And, as instinctive as her love for the baby was, each time she looked at him the knife inside her twisted—because he was the physical manifestation of all that had hurt her and all that was lost to her for ever.

Pain squeezed the fragmented pieces of her heart. She felt confused. And guilty. Because whilst she would never have wished harm on her sister—least of all such a violent death, leaving a baby without his mother and a husband without his wife—there was also an undeniable element of relief. After a lifetime on the receiving end of Julia's bullying and vindictiveness she was now free. Except she wasn't. Not entirely. Because she was still living with the consequences of Julia's actions and manipulations.

Having freshened up, she brushed her hair and retied her ponytail, her thoughts straying back to the previous August, when Gus had arrived at Strathlochan Hospital. Apart from the obvious zing of physical attraction, Gus's eyes had captivated her. Not just their unusual and compelling shade of smoky green, but their expression the first time he'd met her gaze. She'd seen past the guardedness and stony reserve to the inner aloneness. Something had caused that distrust, wariness and soul-deep pain in his eyes.

She'd been drawn to him from the first moment. Not only was he gorgeous to look at, but she'd been impressed by his innate care for his patients. Over those first days and weeks his green eyes had looked at her in ways that had made her heart race and her spine tingle, firing her with a searing desire she'd never experienced before. She had suddenly been so excited about the future.

Until the night of their first date.

A date that had never happened …

Having taken ages to get ready, she'd been buzzing with nervous excitement and on the point of leaving the house when a text had arrived from Gus. That he was cancelling at the very last minute had been a bitter blow, but she'd known he'd been unwell, so she'd set her crashing disappointment aside, concerned instead for his welfare. Her reply had been met with silence and she'd heard nothing more until she'd arrived at work the next day.

The A&E department—indeed, the whole hospital—had been abuzz with gossip and speculation. A shiver of anxiety had rippled down her spine when she'd noticed her colleagues watching her with sympathy and a measure of ghoulish anticipation, but it was when she'd learned the nature of the gossip that her world had fallen apart.

'What happened to your date last night, Holly?' her friend and fellow nurse Kelly Young had asked as they'd changed into scrubs in the locker room.

Holly had tried to manufacture a smile. 'We postponed it. Gus wasn't feeling well,' she explained, unable to mask her disappointment.

'Is that what he told you?' Olivia Barr queried, her tone matching the smirk on her face. 'He was well enough to entertain your sister last night. He and Julia were all over each other and left together to go to his room!' the department's least popular nurse continued with evident enjoyment.

'Julia was seen leaving after breakfast this morning, but Gus has phoned in saying he's too ill to work today. I'm not surprised, given the night he must have had!'

'That's enough, Olivia. You don't have to rub it in,' Kelly reprimanded, leaping to her defence. After Olivia flounced out, she added, 'You know what Olivia's like, Holly, so don't let her nastiness get to you. We're all on your side.'

Holly tried to smile but the damage had been done. She felt sick to her stomach and it took a supreme effort of will not to show her real feelings in front of Olivia. She didn't want to give her gossipy colleague the satisfaction of seeing how upset she was at the news of Gus's betrayal. More than anything she wanted to disbelieve Olivia's words, but as more staff came forward to confirm what they had seen at the Strathlochan Arms, the more wretched, hurt and angry Holly felt.

Julia acting that way was no surprise; it was far from the first time that her sister had hurt her—although this betrayal cut more deeply than the rest. However, it was the realisation that Gus had not only lied to her, but had staged a public rejection of her—and with Julia, of all people—that

ripped her heart to shreds. He must have known
the consequences—that his assignation would be
the talk of the hospital and that not only would
she find out but she'd be plunged into the midst
of gossip.

How could he have done it?

To this day the question still hammered inside her. She'd played second fiddle to Julia all
her life. Her sister had been the pretty one, the
one who could turn on the charm and guile to
get what she wanted, regardless of the hurt she'd
caused along the way. Given past history, Holly
had been scared of Gus and Julia meeting—of
Julia going after Gus and turning his head. And
now her fears had been realised. One look at Julia
and Gus had been ready and willing to cast aside
their friendship, and in doing so had proved that
he hadn't cared about her at all.

Holly rubbed her hands along her arms, feeling the chill despite the warmth in the room. If
she'd thought that first day had been terrible, it
had been nothing compared to the next day when
Gus had returned to work.

The atmosphere in the department had been
electric, Holly recalled, with everyone waiting

for the moment she and Gus came face to face. She bit her lip, failing to force back the memories and the sting of tears that threatened even now. Gus *had* looked terrible, his face unnaturally pale and drawn, making it clear the virus had been genuine and had taken its toll. But she had been too hurt and angry to rustle up much sympathy for him. He'd been well enough to reject her and replace her the same night with her sister, making her the town's laughing stock.

How had Gus expected her to feel? Or hadn't he even thought of her at all? She'd been so furious, so humiliated, so wounded that she hadn't been able to bring herself to look at him. Knowing everyone was watching them and waiting for something to happen, she'd tried hard to avoid him, but every moment had been a strain and it had been inevitable their paths would cross eventually.

'We need to talk, Holly,' Gus had murmured quietly, catching her alone in the plaster room.

'There's nothing to talk about,' she'd responded, with as much calm as she could muster, hurrying to finish her tasks, aware someone could walk in at any moment. 'Nothing you say will change what you did.'

His eyes narrowed and his jaw tightened. 'Well, I have some questions for you. Why did you fail to mention Julia—your *sister*? Or tell me about Euan?'

'That has nothing to do with it.' Holly flinched as he flung the names at her. That Julia had clearly told him about Euan was mortifying. And she knew it wouldn't have been the truthful version. Hurt beyond bearing, she was affronted that Gus should try to pin the blame for his own behaviour on her. Shaking with emotion, and desperate to escape him, she opened the door, unable to keep her voice controlled. 'I trusted you. I thought you were different. But I was wrong. So wrong.' Guilt flashed across his face and, hardening her broken heart against him, she forced herself to continue. 'It's over—whatever *it* was to you. We have nothing more to say to each other.'

'Holly...'

As Gus followed her out of the plaster room Holly closed her ears to the plea in his voice as he called her name. She was conscious of people looking at them and, feeling used and foolish, she wanted a hole to open up and swallow her.

'You've made your choice, now live with it.'

She turned and looked at him one final time. 'You and Julia deserve each other.'

Somehow she'd choked out the words, refusing to cry in front of him, and then she'd turned and walked away.

As the days had passed things at work had remained strained, making her long for the moment when some new scandal would come along to occupy the gossips and remove her from the spotlight. She'd felt pinned down under a microscope, especially during the unavoidable occasions when she and Gus had been called on to work together. They'd been icily polite and starkly professional, but the tension had been palpable, affecting not just Gus and herself but the whole department. Although her colleagues had meant well, and had been nothing but supportive of her, leaving her in no doubt that they held Gus to blame, she knew the situation couldn't continue indefinitely.

She hadn't believed it possible that things could get worse, but she'd been wrong—as she'd discovered when things had come to a head a few weeks later and Julia turned up at the hospital. The buzz in the A&E department had increased to such an extent that the very air had crackled with electricity. Julia had looked beautiful, but fragile—the epitome of male fantasies. Gus had seemed stunned and embarrassed by her arrival…but that had been nothing compared to his shocked expression of horror when Julia had announced for all to hear that she was pregnant.

Holly had felt the news like a hammer-blow. It had left her devastated, angry, humiliated, jealous and confused. Confused because Julia had made her views on babies and motherhood all too clear in the past, so why was she accepting it now? The only explanation Holly had been able to come up with was that her sister must really be in love with Gus to have had such a total change of heart.

As for Gus, knowing what she did of his background, Holly had no doubt how he would react. Whether the baby had been planned or not, Gus would embrace the responsibility of fatherhood one hundred percent.

The flash of triumph in her sister's hazel eyes when Holly had met her gaze had cut her to the quick and confirmed what she had suspected…

Julia had known exactly what she was doing and how much hurt she was inflicting.

Unable to watch them together, or to offer any words of congratulation, Holly had slipped away, seeking privacy before the tears that had threatened to flow could escape. The pain, emptiness and jealousy eating her away had been acute as she'd faced the stark reality: her sister now had everything that Holly had so craved and now lost…Gus and his baby.

News of the pregnancy had been swiftly followed by a rushed December wedding. Holly had been as unsurprised that Gus had demanded it as she'd been surprised that Julia—formerly so anti-marriage—had agreed. But she'd stayed away from the small civil ceremony—as had the entire A&E staff. However, the upsetting chain of events had spurred her to regain control of her own destiny and change things, which had involved putting in a request to transfer to the Children's Ward as early in the New Year as possible, thus removing herself from A&E…and from Gus.

And now Julia was gone.

There was nothing she could do about the past,

Holly allowed, except learn from her mistakes of placing her trust in people who let her down and hurt her so badly. She had to look to the future—especially the future of her nephew. The reality of his existence brought back the painful ache of emptiness that had never really left her, along with a deep sense of loss that made part of her want to run away and never see Gus or his baby again.

But the other part of her had experienced a deep welling of love and protectiveness the instant she had seen the tiny bruised baby—emotions that had only intensified once she'd held him. There had been an instinctive and powerful sense of bonding. And, however difficult and painful life was going to be, she knew in her fractured heart that she could never turn her back on her precious, motherless nephew.

How was Gus going to manage the tiny baby on his own? That question had sparked a range of ideas that had been brewing in her mind since they had first learned of Julia's tragic death and the baby's miraculous fight for life. What she didn't know was how her suggestions might be received—or even, given the bad blood between them, if Gus would listen to her, let alone allow her any kind of role in his son's life.

Leaving the restroom and returning to the main unit, Holly squared her shoulders and sucked in a deep, steadying breath. The days and weeks ahead were not going to be easy, she knew that— both because of the anger and resentment she still felt towards Gus and because of the bittersweet emotions the baby aroused within her. But, whatever the cost to herself, fighting for her nephew was one battle she was determined *not* to lose.

As she approached the section of PICU that housed baby Buchanan she saw that Gus was not alone. One of the nurses was writing up notes while an older woman, who wasn't wearing a uniform, was talking to Gus. Judging from the expression on his face he was far from pleased with what she was saying. Concerned, Holly joined them, ready to help if she could.

'Is there a problem?' she asked, keeping her voice calm and neutral.

Gus's stormy green gaze met hers. 'Holly, this is Alison Davison. She works here in the hospital and liaises with the social workers and health visitors.'

'Ms Davison,' she greeted her politely, setting down her bag and shaking the woman's hand. Alison Davison was in her late forties, Holly guessed; tall and solid-looking, with short dark hair and brown eyes devoid of warmth. 'I'm Holly Tait.'

'You're a relative?' the woman queried.

'I'm the baby's aunt.'

It was the simplest explanation—she couldn't force out the words *sister-in-law* to describe her link to Gus. Still unsure why Alison Davison was there, what had been discussed, and why Gus was looking so furious, Holly instinctively moved closer to him, wanting to present a united front.

'Ms Davison is questioning my ability to care for my son,' Gus explained, his voice carefully controlled but no less lethal for it. 'She wants to know if I'm giving him up for adoption.'

CHAPTER FIVE

'I'VE never heard anything so ridiculous!' Outraged, both at the woman's question and at the insensitive timing of her visit, Holly turned more fully to face her adversary. '*Of course* the baby is going to stay with his father. There's no one better able to care for his son than Gus. How could you ever think he would give up his child?'

Ms Davison crossed her arms defensively across her chest. 'I merely commented that it isn't easy for a man on his own—' she began, but the words only fuelled Holly's anger.

'It's not easy for a woman alone, either, but I don't suppose you go along to visit *them* within hours of their babies arriving and ask if *they've* thought about adoption.'

'No, of course not, and this isn't an official visit. My intention was only to introduce myself. But—'

'Be that as it may,' Holly persisted, warming

to her argument and prepared to do anything to protect her beautiful nephew, 'Gus isn't alone. He has a hospital full of friends who will rally round to help him in any way they can. And then there's me.' Feeling Gus's gaze on her, she sucked in a breath and pressed ahead while she had the chance. 'I'm family. I'll do whatever is necessary to support Gus—including moving into his house to help care for the baby.'

'What about work? Both of you have demanding jobs,' the annoying woman pointed out, apparently determined only to see problems.

Holly wanted to stamp her foot in frustration. 'It's not rocket science! We'll stagger our hours, ensuring that one of us is always there for the baby. And friends will willingly cover any occasional gaps. I doubt many new parents have such a well-qualified pool of babysitters to call on as Gus has.'

'Well, you seem determined. I can see you've thought it all out.' Alison Davison's disappointment was evident, but thankfully she seemed ready to admit defeat. 'I'll leave you my card in case there's anything I can do for you.'

Holly was unsurprised but secretly delighted

when Gus threw the card away before the woman's retreating figure had disappeared from view. Still wearing his scrubs, he looked rumpled and exhausted, a shadow of stubble darkening his jaw. His green gaze shifted, holding her own captive, and Holly swallowed, hoping she hadn't overstepped the mark in her response to Alison Davison.

As the silence lengthened, and he continued to regard her with that brooding expression, her nervousness increased. What was he thinking? He looked wary and suspicious, and his lack of trust in her, proving again how far things had broken down between them, made her unutterably sad. It also made her anxious about how they would work together in the days and weeks ahead. Always assuming Gus was prepared to allow her a role in the baby's life.

A sigh shuddered from her. However impossible it might prove to be for her to be around Gus so much, she had to set her personal issues aside and do what was best. Best for her nephew…and best for the man she had never been able to stop loving.

* * *

'Did you mean what you said?' Gus queried, cautious and uncertain, taken aback by the way Holly had rushed into battle, giving him such vehement support. Again she had appeared genuine and sincere, leaving him even more confused. 'About wanting to move in and be involved with the baby, I mean?'

Sky-blue eyes reflected a flicker of the fiery passion with which she'd faced down Alison Davison. 'Of course I meant it! I know I rushed ahead without consulting you, but she just made me so mad.'

Gus couldn't prevent an inner flash of amusement. Oh, had she been mad! He'd never seen her like that before.

'You ought to report her for what she said, and the thoughtless timing of her visit. It's early days,' she continued, moderating her tone, 'and you haven't had time to think, but living in as I suggested makes sense, Gus...doesn't it?'

Unfortunately it *did* make sense. He dragged the fingers of one hand through his hair, feeling tired and drained after the shocking events of the last hours. It seemed a lifetime ago that he'd first learned of the accident, and so much had happened since then... The terrifying wait for news of whether or not his baby was alive; meeting the neonatal consultant Mr Haggerty; confirmation that there was no hope for Julia; seeing his son for the first time. On top of all that had been various to-ings and fro-ings of doctors, nurses and policemen with their questions. The last thing he had needed was Alison Davison's ill-advised visit.

In the days ahead there would be more on the investigation from the police liaison officer assigned to the case, and more from the doctors on the baby's medical condition. For now, though, they were free of outside interventions. Apart from the dedicated nurses on duty it was just him and his son. And Holly.

He sat down, watching as Holly moved back to her own chair, a smile transforming her face as she leaned forward and slid a hand inside the cot. A little gasp of delight escaped her as the sleeping baby automatically curled his tiny but perfectly formed hand around one of her fingers. Something raw, powerful and dangerous churned inside him as he took in the tableau in front of him.

It was true Holly had shown no interest in his son before, so what had changed? And could he trust her? He didn't know what lay behind her suggestions, but counteracting his doubts was the knowledge that Holly was an excellent nurse; he'd seen that for himself during the time they'd worked together.

There was no question whatsoever of him giving up his son, so he had to be realistic…however much he wanted to, he couldn't do everything alone. He didn't want to bring in a stranger, and in Holly he would have someone with skills in both children's and trauma nursing—plus she was apparently willing to help. He hadn't yet considered all the ramifications, but the most sensible idea *would* be for Holly to move into his house…at least for the time being. It was the last thing he wanted. But *his* wants didn't matter. The baby's did. And if being forced into close proximity with Holly was right for his child in these early formative weeks and months, then he'd just have to find a way to live with it and make it work.

'All right. We'll try it.' His agreement was tentative and reluctant, the decision made for his son's sake, not his own.

'Thank you.' The words were brief and she kept her gaze averted, so he was unable to gauge her real feelings. 'Have you considered a name, Gus?'

Holly's question changed the direction of his thoughts and he looked at his tiny son, marvelling anew at the perfection of him: the cap of soft, downy light brown hair on his head, the little movements of his mouth as he slept, the beat of his heart so visible under the almost translucent skin of his chest. Love welled within him, along with knowledge of the magnitude of the responsibilities that lay ahead.

'I hate to keep referring to him as *"the baby"*,' Holly added, gently fingering the security band around his son's fragile wrist, which simply read, 'Baby Buchanan'.

'No decision was made regarding names,' he answered gruffly.

In truth he hadn't given it much thought, because Julia had been determined that *she* would decide. It had been one of many points of contention, but at the time it hadn't seemed imminently important, and he'd refused to be drawn into an argument when Julia had come up with ever more ridiculous names, inspired by the celebrity trend for the weird and unusual.

'I don't mean to intrude, but I have an idea if you'd care to hear it…one that I think means something to you and has resonance with both sides of the baby's family.'

The nervousness and reticence in Holly's voice suggested she was treading on eggshells around him. Weary, but grateful for the support she'd shown him, he made an effort to be less brusque with her.

'Tell me,' he invited, earning himself the barest flicker of a smile.

'I was thinking…' She paused, glancing at him uncertainly before returning her gaze to the sleeping form in the cot. 'If you don't like it, that's fine—you choose whatever you want—but I came up with Max. Maxwell Angus Tait Buchanan.'

A fist clenched inside him as the full impact of Holly's proposition sank in. She'd not only remembered something he'd told her ten months earlier, but she'd grasped its significance. The Christian name belonged to the only person who had meant anything in his life before he'd come to Strathlochan.

Maxwell McTavish. The teacher who had looked past the exterior and seen the boy within. He'd become his mentor and confidant, encouraging him to fulfil his potential and helping him believe in himself. Maxwell's sudden death four years ago had left him distraught, Gus admitted, choking up with the memories.

Apart from Maxwell, Holly was the only other person he'd ever trusted, talked to or allowed into his heart. He still didn't understand the intense connection between them during his first weeks in Strathlochan, but he'd shared things with Holly that he'd never revealed to another living soul. Not even Maxwell. And, despite recent hostilities, Holly had suggested the one name guaranteed to touch his emotions.

'You remembered,' he murmured, his voice hoarse.

'Yes.' Her eyes were huge as she looked at him—huge and filled with doubt. 'If you don't like it—'

'I do.' He shook his head to get rid of the confusion. Of course he liked it. He couldn't have picked anything better himself. He met her gaze, not caring for that brief moment what he revealed to her. 'Thank you, Holly.'

He saw her swallow, saw the sheen of moisture that clouded her eyes, and his heart turned over when she produced the first natural smile he'd seen from her in months. A smile that dimpled her cheeks, squeezed his heart and turned his insides to mush.

Relieved by Gus's reaction to her idea about the name, Holly was moved by the emotion he revealed to her, reminding her of the old Gus—*her* Gus—in the days when they'd shared a special closeness. At least on her side. She was no longer sure Gus had felt anything. Maybe she'd just deluded herself that he'd felt something for her because she'd so desperately wanted him to.

She'd been scared to mention the name, unsure if Gus would find her suggestion intrusive. She knew what Maxwell McTavish had meant to him, just as she understood why family was so important...the reason she'd known he would move heaven and earth for his child. And she knew all this because, days after they'd met, he'd told her about his life and Maxwell's place in it.

'How long have you lived in Strathlochan?' Gus had asked as they'd sat outside having a late lunch after a busy morning in A&E.

'All my life,' she'd told him, licking some stray mayonnaise from her tuna sandwich off her fingers. 'I was born and raised here. My dad died when I was sixteen, which was really hard, and I stayed with my mum at home while I did my nursing training—which was good, because I was able to take care of her when she became ill.'

Gus had been sympathetic, listening as if what she'd said was important to him. Encouraged by his attention, she'd opened up and shared some of her childhood memories…ones that didn't include Julia. He hadn't asked if she had any siblings, and that suited her just fine. The longer she kept Julia a secret the better.

'Do you still live in the house?' he'd asked.

'No, it had to be sold after Mum died.' She'd struggled to control her emotions, hiding the real reason she'd had to say goodbye to the home she loved. 'That's when I moved in with George. I've been there ever since.'

Gus's mood had changed in an instant, his face tightening, long lashes lowering to mask the expression in his eyes. 'Oh, right. Sorry, I didn't realise.'

'Realise what?' she'd asked, confused by the sudden change in him and the flat, distant tone of his voice.

'That you were involved with someone.'

'Involved?' she'd repeated with a puzzled frown.

Sighing, Gus had sat back on the bench, hands thrust into the pockets of his scrub trousers as he'd gazed up at the blue sky dotted with puffy white clouds. 'George.'

'Oh!' She hadn't been able to prevent a giggle escaping as the misunderstanding had become clear. 'George as in Georgia Millar…she's a staff nurse on the Children's Ward!'

His answering chuckle had been laden with relief and a hint of embarrassment. 'Right…that's good! I've probably seen her around the hospital, but I can't put a face to the name,' he'd responded, finishing his sandwich with renewed appetite.

The knowledge that he'd been upset at the

thought of her with another man had brought a warm glow and a tingle of excitement as she'd dared to hope he might like her as much as she liked him.

'George lost her dad shortly before my mum died. Since then she's rented out rooms in her house,' Holly had explained. 'Kelly—as in Kelly Young from A&E—lives there, too.'

'Is that something you thought of doing in your own home?'

Gus's question had hit a raw nerve, and she'd looked away lest he read the emotions in her eyes. She'd shaken her head, declining to explain why his suggestion wouldn't have worked for her as it had so successfully for George. Doing so would have meant telling him about Julia, and that had been a road she hadn't wanted to travel.

'How about you, Gus?' she'd asked, moving the conversation away from herself. She'd more or less fallen in love with Gus from day one and wanted to find out all about him. 'What's your family like?'

'I don't know…I've never had one.'

Her bottle of juice had remained suspended in mid-air, part-way to her mouth, untasted and forgotten. She'd turned to face Gus, shocked not only by his words but by the bleak emptiness in his voice. Unable to stop herself, she'd reached out her free hand to take one of his, their fingers naturally entwining.

'How do you mean?' The question whispered from her, and she felt a mix of trepidation and suspense as she waited for him to answer, fearful for several long, tense moments that he'd shut himself away and not confide in her. 'Gus…?'

A jagged breath shuddered from him and he sat forward, his gaze averted, his fingers clinging to hers as if to a lifeline. Her drink set aside, Holly held on tight with both hands, willing him to talk, but increasingly fearful of what he might say.

'I was abandoned outside a hospital in Glasgow one frosty March morning,' he began, and Holly barely contained her gasp of shock. 'A nurse found me and rushed me inside. I was only a few hours old. They treated me for near hypothermia, and it was touch and go for a while whether I'd develop pneumonia or some other breathing problem. I didn't. An appeal went out for my mother to come forward—there were concerns for her own health, physical and mental—but she never did. And a police enquiry proved fruitless.'

A shiver ran through her at the cold, emotionless tone of his voice. 'Wh-What happened to you?' she managed, stunned by the image of Gus as a baby, abandoned in the cold.

'The nurse who found me named me Angus, but I've no idea where Buchanan came from.' He paused, glancing briefly in her direction, and Holly squeezed his hand supportively. 'When I was well enough to leave hospital I was placed in foster care,' he continued, fledgling emotion beginning to challenge the dispassionate nature of his account. 'It became one foster home after another for the first few years until I was finally placed in a children's home, age six, labelled difficult and unable to settle.'

'How could any child settle in circumstances like that?' Holly exclaimed, incapable of containing her reaction, furious and hurting for the little boy who had been passed from pillar to post for so many years. Of *course* he hadn't been able to put down roots. He must have felt unloved and frightened, and horribly let down by a system designed to help which, in his case, had failed abysmally.

'I don't know. I certainly didn't. Not that the home was any better,' he admitted, and she could feel the shudder that ran through him as he faced his memories. 'I hated it there.'

Holly struggled to keep her tears for him at bay. 'How long were you there?'

'Until I was sixteen.'

'All that time?' she responded, unable to keep a horrified gasp in check. 'What about adoption? Why didn't they help find you a loving family?'

His expression hardened, but she saw the hurt and loneliness in his eyes before he looked away. 'They tried…but no one wanted me.'

'Oh, Gus,' she whispered, a tear escaping.

'Don't cry for me.' The fingers of his free hand gently wiped her cheek. 'I survived. And when I started senior school I met Maxwell McTavish.'

As a smile stripped the harshness from his face Holly latched onto the information he'd given. 'He was a teacher?' she asked, anxious to learn more, to hear what had shaped him into the man he was today.

'Yes. He saw something in me and had the patience and dedication to burrow past the angry, defensive exterior I'd cultivated to find it. He's the nearest thing I ever had to a father. It's thanks to him that education became my way out and gave me a chance to make something of myself.'

He let out a deep breath, and she wanted to hug the man for giving Gus the care and encouragement he'd badly needed.

'He sounds amazing.'

'He was,' Gus allowed, a waver in his voice, his smile fading.

Heart in her mouth, she whispered the question that hung in the air. 'Was?'

'Was.' Gus swallowed, emotion thickening his voice, his fingers once more tightening on hers. 'He died four years ago—a sudden massive stroke. He was only fifty-four. I never had the chance to say goodbye or to thank him. And he never saw me qualify as a doctor.'

Uncaring who saw them, or what anyone thought, Holly wrapped her arms around him, fresh tears squeezing between her lashes. Having lost her own father suddenly, she knew how Gus must have felt about Maxwell, the man who had fulfilled Gus's need to feel loved and to belong.

'I'm sure he knew how you felt. And he'd be so very proud of you, Gus. You're a credit to him,' she murmured, her own emotions showing as she attempted to comfort him, her tears dampening the top of his scrubs.

'Thank you, Holly.'

As they finished their lunch he told her more about Maxwell, and then he spoke of his feelings growing up alone, of what the idea of family meant to him.

'I have no idea what the future holds in store,' he concluded, 'but if I'm ever lucky enough to have a child I intend to make damn sure he or she knows exactly where they've come from, and is raised in a proper family with the love of a mother and a father and everything else I missed out on.'

Knowing about his past meant she'd understood Gus's reaction to Julia's pregnancy, but that hadn't made his rejection of her in favour of her slender, beautiful sister any less painful. Nor had it eased the bitter regret and jealousy… More than anything, *she'd* wanted to be the woman to give Gus the family and the love he'd craved, and to be the mother of his children. But Gus's decision to build that family with Julia had shattered her hopes…and her heart.

Now Julia had been violently taken from him, wrecking his dream of building his own family and leaving his son without a mother. Gus didn't want her; he'd made that clear. But even though he'd hurt her, and she hated what he'd done, she wanted to help provide a loving, stable world for Max.

Regrouping, she turned back to her nephew. 'Maxwell Angus Tait Buchanan seems far too big a name for such a tiny person,' she admitted with a nervy laugh, moved by the memory of the time Gus had confided in her, and sorrowful that the trust and closeness they'd shared had evaporated so completely.

'He'll grow into it,' Gus responded with a tired half-smile, his gaze on his sleeping son.

'Please God, let's hope so.' She paused a moment before softly voicing her fear. 'Max will be all right, Gus, won't he?'

Gus looked up. Holly's sky-blue eyes were huge and full of anxiety. The feeling in her voice called to him, and without conscious thought he did what she'd done for him earlier in the day: he took her free hand in his, understanding the basic human need for contact and comfort. He didn't answer because he didn't know what to say, and he didn't want to tempt fate. Like Holly, he'd experienced myriad emotions about Max's immediate future.

For long moments they sat in silence, watching Max, listening to the buzz of the unit and the bleeping of the monitors. The highly skilled nurses cared for their tiny charges with dedication, kindness and efficiency. Gus looked around the unit. Each cot contained a fragile, often precarious new life, just like Max, watched over by parents who felt the same worries he and Holly shared.

'You look exhausted,' Holly murmured with concern. 'If you want to go and freshen up, maybe get changed and have something to eat, I won't leave Max.'

He knew she was right. Hell, he was still in the scrubs he'd pulled on in A&E who knew how many hours ago? He released her hand, immediately missing the feel of her soft skin.

'There are so many things to think about…

things to do that haven't even occurred to me yet,' he admitted, barely realising that in his tiredness he was slipping back into the old habit of confiding in Holly.

'I know. And it isn't easy. I'm so sorry, Gus. I wish you didn't have to face all this.' Understanding vied with the anxiety in her eyes. 'I had to take care of all the formalities alone after my mum died, so I know what it's like.'

'And Julia?'

Holly looked down, hiding her expression from him. 'She wasn't around at the time.'

'Not for her own mother?'

He failed to mask his disbelief, and this time Holly's lashes lifted, her startled gaze clashing with his. 'You didn't know?'

'Know what?' he asked in puzzlement.

'Julia and I were half-sisters,' she explained, surprising him anew.

And yet it immediately made so much sense. He forced himself to concentrate as Holly continued.

'Julia's mum Marie died when Julia was three. Dad met and married my mother soon afterwards, and within the year they had me. It must have been a huge upheaval for a little girl, not under-standing where her mother had gone or why the father she doted on hadn't as much time for her.'

'And then a new woman and a new baby came along in quick succession?' he added, leaning forward and resting his elbows on his knees.

'Exactly,' Holly agreed with a small, sad smile, evidently hurting for the little girl her sister had once been. 'It's not surprising Julia's nose was put out of joint.'

It explained a great deal, and Gus wondered what lasting effects those early years had had on Julia. And on her relationship with Holly. It was clear he had much yet to discover, and it threw him into even greater confusion.

'Let me know if you'd like some company while you're dealing with the official paperwork and things,' Holly volunteered, reclaiming his attention. 'And if there's anything else I can do to help…'

'Thanks.'

He shouldn't take Holly up on her offer. The less time he spent in her company the better—especially while he reinforced his defences ready for when Max came home and Holly moved in.

But his new responsibilities weighed heavily upon him, and the prospect of making all the decisions, including funeral arrangements, was unappealing. He was used to being alone. He always had been. But whatever difficulties lay between Holly and himself—and, as he was discovering, between Holly and Julia—she still had a right to be involved in organising the funeral.

'It's not only the official stuff. There'll be preparations for Max,' Holly added.

Gus nodded. 'I thought I had another month to get ready. There's so much to do. I haven't started the nursery yet,' he confessed, declining to mention the number of times Julia had changed her mind about what she wanted.

'I have time off. I'd be happy to paint Max's room,' Holly offered tentatively.

He'd be mad to turn her down, Gus knew. He needed all the help he could get. But… Stifling a sigh, he ran a hand through his wayward hair. It seemed pointless, worrying about spending time in her company when he'd agreed for her to move into his house. However temporarily. It was the most sensible option, and the best thing for Max, but that didn't make him like it.

'If you don't want me to—'

'No, I do.' Holly's words brought his rushed denial. He needed the help, and if he planned well he could ensure he was out when she was there. 'I'd appreciate it—thanks.'

She smiled shyly. 'OK. Have you any idea how you want the nursery to be?'

'Not really. It was Julia's domain—' He broke off and they looked at each other, the silence tense as reality sank in. 'You do what you think is best.'

With the atmosphere between them less adversarial than it had been in months, Gus rose to his feet. He hated leaving Max, even briefly, but he needed a shower and a change of clothes. His stomach rumbled, making him realise how long it was since he'd eaten.

'I won't be long,' he said, feeling awkward again.

Holly glanced round and gave a distracted nod before refocusing on Max. 'I'm not going anywhere.'

No. They were stuck with each other…for the time being. As he walked away, Gus reflected on the vagaries of Fate and how quickly life could change. Julia had sparked off a chain of events that had ended tragically for her yet miraculously had delivered him his son. But it had also brought Holly back into his life. And he had no idea what the future held in store—for either of them.

CHAPTER SIX

As HE poured milk into three mugs of tea, Gus looked back on the last couple of days. They'd passed in a blur of activity, with meetings, shopping and preparations, on top of spending as much time with Max as possible. He was glad of the hectic whirl…it gave him little time to brood over things.

Namely: Holly.

Whilst the reserve and awkwardness persisted, true to her word she'd remained constant in her support of him and her devotion to his son. Both he and Holly had been offered compassionate leave from the hospital. With the understanding and influence of their heads of department arrangements were being made to stagger their hours when they returned to work, cutting down the times they might need to ask friends to babysit.

That was in the future. The immediate priority was to prepare for Max's homecoming. In the last two days, as well as shopping for supplies to decorate the nursery, they'd taken care of the official paperwork regarding Julia's death and Max's birth, and visited the funeral director to make arrangements to lay Julia to rest. Discovering that Holly was as keen as he to keep things simple had brought huge relief. The police had released Julia's body, and they'd planned the funeral for Monday: both of them wanted to put that difficult event behind them before Max left the hospital.

Gus carried the mugs through to the living room and handed one to Holly and one to Officer Bruce Gourlay, the family liaison police officer assigned to them. Sitting down, Gus felt edgy and on high alert—partly due to Holly being in his home for the first time, and partly at waiting to hear if Bruce had answers to some of the questions about Julia's accident.

'Firstly I can tell you that technicians have examined your car and found no mechanical faults or defects…nothing to cause an accident,' Bruce informed them. 'There were no skid marks on the road. I'm sorry, but all the evidence suggests that under the influence of alcohol Julia either fell asleep at the wheel or her concentration was otherwise impaired.'

'I can't understand why she took the car.' Gus frowned, shaking his head. 'She must have taken the spare keys from my desk—it was no secret they were there—but anyway I didn't think she had a licence.'

'She did, but...'

As Holly's words trailed off Gus looked at her, noting the way she set down her mug and clasped her hands in her lap, nibbling her lip in apparent uncertainty. Clearly she knew something. Something she felt uncomfortable revealing. But what? And if it was important why hadn't she spoken up before?

'But what?' he prompted, trying not to let his impatience show.

'Julia *did* have a driving licence, but she racked up penalty points on it,' she informed them. A sigh escaped and she shook her head. 'Last July she was stopped for drink-driving,' she continued, her voice filled with emotion. 'She lost her licence for twelve months, so she wouldn't have been due to apply for a replacement until August or September—I don't know the exact date. Whatever possessed her to drive, and to drink—especially given her pregnancy? She must have known she wouldn't have insurance while banned.'

An electric silence hummed in the room. As he digested Holly's explanation Gus was aware once more of how little he had known his unfortunate wife. Or Holly. How many more things had the sisters hidden from him?

'Does the name Dalziel mean anything to either of you?' Bruce asked now, cutting across his introspection.

'Not to me,' Holly replied with a frown.

Gus shook his head. 'Nor me. Why?'

'We found an order of service sheet in Julia's bag,' the officer explained. 'Paul Dalziel, a financier from Edinburgh, and his wife Claudia, were killed in a light plane crash nearly two weeks ago. Their joint funeral was held on Wednesday.'

The day Julia died, Gus realised immediately. 'And is that where Julia had been?'

'Yes,' Bruce confirmed, reaching for the file that lay on the sofa cushion beside him. 'The Dalziels' three children, all young adults, didn't recognise Julia, and have no idea of her connection to their parents. Witnesses at the funeral came forward in response to appeals for help with our enquiries and confirmed Julia was there.'

As the policeman opened the file and consulted the papers within Gus puzzled over the new information. Who were the Dalziels? And if they were so important to her why had Julia never mentioned them to him? Or to Holly, who appeared as much in the dark as he was? He had no answers, and frustration mounted.

Setting his mug aside, Bruce continued. 'Julia was reported to have been extremely upset. Although no one remembers talking to her, several people recall her drinking heavily. They noticed, of course, in particular because she was heavily pregnant,' he added with a shake of his head.

Whatever sympathy Gus had for Julia's grief was overridden by his disgust and anger at the inexcusable way she'd risked their baby's life— and the lives of other innocent people—by drink-driving. While banned. If only someone had challenged her, perhaps the tragedy would have been avoided. If only…

'We also have an independent witness who

had a lucky escape when he managed to avoid a collision with Julia shortly before the accident. Apparently she ran a red light and pulled out of a junction in front of him,' Bruce explained. 'He said she seemed severely emotionally distressed and wasn't concentrating on the road. He immediately called the police to report the incident, giving the registration number and location, and was extremely concerned by Julia's obvious lack of control.'

Gus was thankful that someone, at least, had tried to do something. It had been too late for the police to stop Julia before the accident. It was a miracle no one else had been hurt—or worse. Julia had paid the ultimate price. And he'd come far too close to losing his son.

The official accident report, Bruce went on, revealed that Julia hadn't worn a seatbelt. Her judgement impaired, her reactions and decisions adversely affected by her emotional state and the alcohol, she hadn't stood a chance. The miracle was Max. There Fate *had* been kind. Gus felt forever indebted to Frazer, Rick and the hospital specialists whose efforts had saved his baby's life.

He had another issue to resolve, Gus realised, turning his attention to more mundane matters. His car was a write-off, and how would the insurance company react when they learned Julia had not only been driving without his permission but without a licence? Could he bear that financial hit along with everything else? He made a mental note to ask the solicitor Holly had named, who was dealing with Julia's affairs.

After Officer Gourlay had left, Gus felt restless. When he'd initially told Holly about the officer's impending visit he'd proposed they go shopping for baby essentials afterwards, but that was the last thing he felt like doing now. He wanted to hold his son.

'Go, Gus. We can shop another time,' Holly offered with gentle understanding.

Her uncanny ability to read his thoughts scared him. 'Are you sure?'

'Of course. This must be impossibly difficult for you.' Her voice wavered, but she took a deep breath and smiled, changing the subject. 'May I make a start on the nursery while you're gone?'

'Of course you can. I'd appreciate it.'

'There's nothing in particular you want done?' she asked again.

'No.' It was one less thing to think about. 'You decide.'

Holly's smile tugged at his gut. 'OK. I have some ideas.'

He pushed his curiosity away, grateful for the help and relieved she'd be working on it while he was out. Gus still felt uneasy in her presence. Part of him regretted agreeing to her moving in when Max came home, but his son came first. And, of course, he was enormously grateful for her kindness and support, however else she made him feel. In any case, he would continue to make whatever sacrifices were necessary to ensure his son's happiness and security.

Max… Emotion welled within him. Through the stress of the past few days his son had kept him going. He was small, but the specialists were increasingly surprised by his strength and rapid recovery. Questions continued to arise about his date of conception. Gus frowned. If he hadn't been one hundred percent certain of the timing he might have had doubts himself, but it was the one thing he *was* positive about. He remembered nothing of the actual event, which increased his feelings of guilt and self-disgust, and he'd been paying for the mistake ever since. But all the trials, upsets and sacrifices had faded into insignificance the instant he'd seen Max and held his bruised little body in his arms for the first time.

The most important thing was that Max survived with as few long-term consequences as possible. And as each day passed it appeared his wish might come true. Max was remarkably resilient, responding well, feeding without problems, and the test results were encouraging—so much so that his son had been dubbed 'the miracle baby' by those involved in his care.

His miracle baby.

Crossing to his desk, he took out a spare set of house keys. 'You'll need these, Holly.'

'Thank you.' She followed him into the hallway. 'Give Max a cuddle from me. I'll see him later.'

Gus hesitated and turned to her, struck by how young she looked, her face bare of make-up, a shaft of sunlight catching the soft waves of her hair and giving it a golden glow. He experienced the same shiver of awareness now that he'd felt the first time he saw her. She'd been unlike anyone he'd ever met before. And from day one she'd befriended him and taken him under her wing.

He never allowed people close—experience had taught him to trust no one but himself. Apart from Maxwell McTavish. So he'd been surprised when he'd bonded instantly with Holly, opening up to her as he never had with anyone before. Which had made her rejection even more agonising.

Pain, loneliness and mistrust swirled within him. Having been duped once by Holly, he intended to guard what remained of his heart.

Shaking off the physical awareness of Holly's presence so close to him, he said a brisk goodbye, stepped outside and closed the door, putting a solid barrier between Holly and himself. A necessary barrier. Because slowly but surely she was breaching his defences again and he couldn't allow that to happen.

Having been given *carte blanche* in decorating the nursery, Holly took great care in bringing her ideas to life. She worked for hours after Gus had left the house on Friday, after meeting Bruce

Gourlay, and solidly over the weekend, too, wanting to finish in time for the room to air before Max came home.

Now it was Monday afternoon and, having spent the morning coping with the ordeal of Julia's funeral, she was putting the finishing touches to the room. She hadn't seen Gus since Friday. Until this morning. As pain squeezed her heart she leaned on the sill, welcoming the gentle breeze through the open window.

The funeral service and the burial that had followed had been simple but dignified. Seeing Julia laid to rest in Strathlochan's churchyard beside her mother and father—with Holly's own mother on the other side—had been emotionally draining, bringing back memories good and bad.

Watching Gus had made her heart ache for him. He'd withdrawn further into himself and, standing across from her, still as a statue, his face had been an unreadable mask, as if hewn from granite. He'd looked gorgeous in a dark suit and tie— gorgeous but unapproachable. His suffering had brought tears to her eyes. However hurt, angry and confused she was by his rejection, she would never have wanted this to happen to him.

George and Kelly had been working, and unable to attend, but Gina and Ruth had been on either side of her, each holding one of her hands, Seb and Rico—the latter having flown over from Italy, which had touched her hugely—had stood behind them, supportive and understanding.

Always unpopular, Julia had barely spent any time in Strathlochan since she'd left home at seventeen, so Holly had been surprised by the number of people present.

'I can't believe how many came,' she'd murmured to her friends as they'd walked back through the churchyard to the lych gate.

'They aren't here for Julia,' Gina had murmured back. 'They're here for *you*, hon. And Gus.'

Gus had stood next to her, shaking hands and thanking people for coming, and she'd sensed his tension as people offered their condolences. Witnessing his grief had left her feeling inept, unable to think of anything to do or say to comfort him and alleviate his sorrow. The cause of his pain intensified her own.

Once everyone had gone apart from Gina, Seb, Ruth and Rico, who'd waited nearby, Holly had laid a hand on Gus's arm.

'Oh, Gus, I'm so sorry.' Her voice had wavered and the breath had locked in her lungs as he'd met her gaze, his deep green eyes cooler and more distant than ever. 'I know how you feel—'

'No, you *don't* know how I feel, Holly,' he'd replied harshly, a bitter, angry edge to his voice as he'd shaken off her hand. 'You have absolutely no idea. You made your position clear months ago. I don't know what you're trying to do now, but it won't work. I don't need you or your crocodile tears.'

She'd stood motionless as Gus had walked away, watching his solitary figure, crushed by his reaction. His accusing words and the angry disgust as he'd uttered them had rung in her ears. As her friends had moved to her side she'd tried to stifle the sob that rose within her. Gus's rejection and the emotion of the occasion had all been too much to bear.

'What happened?' Ruth demanded with a frown.

As Gina put an arm around her Holly haltingly told her friends what Gus had said. 'He looked at me as if he hated me. I don't understand what

I've done or what went so wrong,' she finished brokenly, unable to hold back her hurt.

'Oh, Holly!' Gina exclaimed, hugging her.

Ruth handed her a tissue. 'I don't think for a minute that Gus hates you. He's hurting, and he's just lashing out at whoever is closest.'

'Ruth's right, hon,' Gina stated, with more conviction that Holly could muster. 'And, while I hate to speak ill of the dead, I wouldn't put it past Julia to have painted you in as bad a light as possible to Gus.'

'Maybe...' Holly secretly agreed with her friend's assessment. 'But Gus didn't have to believe it. And what was the point? She'd already won, taken everything I wanted. She had Gus's ring on her finger and was carrying his baby.'

They were silent, lost in thought at the tragic end Julia had faced and the miraculous survival of baby Max.

'Perhaps Julia still felt threatened, knowing how close you and Gus had been and how you felt about him?' Gina sighed, her expression thoughtful. 'I'm worried about you—we all are. Holly, sweetheart, you have to stop breaking your heart over Gus.'

Holly sucked in an unsteady breath, unsure if it was possible for her already shattered heart to break any further. 'It's not like that,' she lied, frightened and despairing, because—despite everything—she loved Gus as much as ever.

She felt guilty for her emotions about Julia. There was deep sorrow, of course, but she couldn't deny the relief after all Julia had done to her. And the anger, not only for endangering her baby but for the ultimate betrayal with Gus.

'I'm such a horrible person,' she whispered as the three of them followed Seb and Rico, who had gone on ahead of them.

'What rubbish!' Gina exclaimed.

'You're the least horrible person I know,' Ruth added, resting an arm around her waist.

Gina nodded in agreement. 'You're feeling a natural human reaction. Julia made your life a misery from childhood. Of course you have mixed feelings. No one thinks badly of you for it...*we* certainly don't.'

'Most people would have given up on Julia years ago,' Ruth pointed out. 'But no matter how much she hurt you, you never turned your back on her.'

Holly closed her eyes, recalling the things Julia had said and done over the years. Pain assailed her as her secret loomed, leaving her feeling empty and hollow. A secret she'd shared with no one—not even Gina, Ruth and George. Besides her GP, only Julia had known, and her callous reaction hurt as much now as it had at the time. It made her sister's final, most wounding betrayal with Gus all the more devastating.

'Ruth's right, hon,' Gina insisted, taking her hand, concern etched on her face. 'Holly, are you sure you're doing the right thing, moving into Gus's house to help with little Max?'

A shiver ran down Holly's spine but she doggedly ignored it. 'It's all I *can* do.'

'It's going to be hard on you,' Gina advised, squeezing her hand.

'I wish I wasn't moving to Italy in August and could stay to support you. Promise you'll ask if there's *anything* I can do,' Ruth instructed, giving her a hug. 'We can't help worrying about you, Holly.'

She was grateful for her friends' care and support. 'I have to do this—for Max, for Gus and for me,' she stated, hiding her doubts and anxieties from them even as a knot of fear and despair tightened its grip. What did the future hold in store?

Now, alone in the nursery, she recalled that conversation. Behind the words and outward smile she was scared witless. It would be horribly awkward moving into this house—the home Gus had shared with Julia. Being around him kept her on a knife-edge of tension as she tried to hide her feelings for him and her hurt confusion at his change in attitude towards her. He might need help with Max, but she had little doubt that accepting it from her was a last resort and done with reluctance. It hurt.

Sighing, she switched on her radio and continued putting the finishing touches to the nursery. Gus hadn't yet seen what she'd done, and she was nervous of his reaction. The nervousness was mixed with uncertainty about facing him again following his parting words at the church. He hadn't returned to the house following the funeral, and she couldn't help but worry about him, hurting for his pain but also pained herself at the distance between them and the knowledge that he'd loved Julia and not her.

Instead she tried to focus on the exciting news that Max was coming home tomorrow—provided Mr Haggerty and his team were happy when they did their morning rounds. Her heart swelled with love every time she thought of him or saw him. However difficult forced proximity with Gus became, she would make the best of it and remind herself of what mattered: Max.

Further questions had been asked about Max's unusual development, but Gus remained adamant about the date of conception. She *so* wanted to believe him. Because, as painful as the knowledge was that Max had been conceived on the night Gus was meant to have been out with *her*, to discover Gus and Julia had been together *before* that would be an even more bitter pill to swallow.

She was on the stepladder, hanging the curtains she'd had made, when she heard the key in the front door. Gus was home. Wariness and anticipation filled her. What would he think of the nursery? Had she gone too far? Would Gus even bother to come upstairs when he realised she was there? A tense knot tightened in her stomach and her fingers shook as she worked her way slowly along the first row of hooks, her senses attuned to the man downstairs.

The bravado and the front of self-confidence with which she'd attempted to fool Gina and Ruth crumbled to dust. She wanted to run away and hide so that Gus couldn't hurt her any more.

Anxious about what would happen when they came face to face again, she waited with bated breath for the sound of his footsteps climbing the stairs.

CHAPTER SEVEN

'DAMN!'

The sound of the radio was the first thing Gus heard as he stepped inside his house and closed the front door behind him.

Holly was in the nursery.

A mix of emotions swirled inside him. The temptation to leave until she went home was huge, but he resisted, knowing it was ridiculous. Not only was it *his* house, but in a matter of hours she would be moving in, and as they shared the responsibility of caring for Max in the forthcoming weeks he would not be able to avoid her for ever.

If she still agreed to the plan. After the way he'd spoken to her at the funeral he wouldn't blame her for avoiding him. He'd been much harsher than he'd intended, his emotions wound taut by the strain of the occasion and trying to maintain the role of grieving husband with the guilt it engendered.

Reluctant to face Holly, he went to the kitchen and took a can of cola from the fridge. He enjoyed a long pull of the icy drink before pressing the can to his forehead, welcoming the coldness against his skin. It had been a hot day…one that had been more difficult than he'd anticipated.

Gus closed his eyes, recalling the ordeal of the funeral. The large turnout had surprised him, while the kindness and sympathy offered by the people present had made him horribly uncomfortable. Their condolences had rendered him awkward and stilted—and incredibly ashamed that it was not grief he felt, as everyone presumed, but relief. Not that Julia was dead—never that—but at being freed from their loveless marriage.

He cursed under his breath. What kind of man was he? They'd both been miserable these last months. He recalled the moment Julia had come to the hospital, tearfully announcing in front of his colleagues—including Holly—that she was pregnant. He'd been stunned. And still unable to remember anything of the night in question. But wishing it wasn't true hadn't made it go away.

He'd shouldered the responsibility, determined to do the right thing.

Julia had wanted someone to take care of her, and after his own unhappy upbringing he'd been adamant his child would never grow up the same way. It had to be legally binding to safeguard his rights to his child and Julia had agreed, however reluctantly, to a marriage in name only.

He couldn't blame people for thinking the marriage had been genuine and he was grief-stricken. And how could he explain the truth without sounding callous? Julia had given him a son. The least he could do was to preserve her memory in the eyes of her family, friends and the community. For Max's sake as well as her own.

He'd given Julia the security, home and money she'd wanted, in return for full responsibility for the baby. They'd lived under the same roof, and in the beginning they'd rubbed along fairly well—if not as friends, then at least with polite tolerance. But the atmosphere had become tense and increasingly hostile as the months went by.

Julia had hated being pregnant. Gus took another drink and opened the kitchen door, welcoming what fresh air there was in the hot summer evening. As a doctor, he'd understood as well as any man could that pregnancy wrought huge changes to a woman—physically and emotionally. Some women breezed through the nine months with few problems, enjoying the whole experience, while others had spells of illness, morning sickness and general bad moods and discomfort. Julia had experienced the worst of everything. He'd tried to make allowances and be patient, but Julia had been difficult to be around. Nothing had suited her and she'd complained constantly. He'd stuck it out…for the baby.

His heart missed a beat as he thought of his beautiful son. How could he regret anything when Max was the result? His childhood had left its mark, and he'd sympathised with Julia when she'd spoken of becoming estranged from her father because of Holly. She hadn't divulged details of the rift, but he'd understood Julia's feeling alone without her family. Now Julia was gone and he was left with Max and the fearful responsibility of learning how to be a father.

Tomorrow he would bring Max home. Part of him was relieved Holly would be around, yet he couldn't help but be wary of her motives. If she *was* putting on an act he'd soon know: she couldn't keep it up indefinitely when living under the same roof.

Unable to avoid her, Gus headed for the stairs, curious to see the nursery. He halted in the doorway, captivated by the sight that greeted him. Holly was balanced on the stepladder, hanging colourful curtains, the material gently fluttering in the welcome breeze through the open windows.

She'd changed out of her dark funeral outfit and was dressed in cut-off faded denim shorts that left her legs bare to mid-thigh. Perfect legs… beautifully shaped and silky smooth. Arousal slammed into him. His gaze roved up the teasing swell of her bottom, outlined by the stone-washed fabric of her shorts. As she stretched to reach the furthest hooks on the curtain rail, the hem of her T-shirt rode up, exposing a tantalising strip of pale gold skin across her lower back.

The lavender-coloured top framed her curves, and as she moved he could see the outline of firm, exquisitely shaped breasts. She wasn't wearing a bra. He forced his reluctant gaze to continue upwards. Her wavy blonde hair was tied in a haphazard ponytail, a few strands escaping to feather her neck and make-up-free face. As he watched her concentrating on her task, her pink tongue-tip peeped out of the corner of her mouth. She looked ridiculously young and innocent and tempting.

Angry, ashamed and confused by his instinctive attraction, Gus ducked back into the hallway and leaned against the landing wall before Holly saw him, taking a moment to regain control before making his presence known. How could he still feel like this about Holly? It was a warning he'd do well to heed if he was to maintain his guard. He didn't want to be fooled and hurt again.

Hearing the stepladder being folded, Gus sucked in a steadying breath and returned to the nursery. Holly was humming along with the music on the radio while she cleared away her things, her back to him. He gave a cough to announce his presence, and she swung round with a little *'Oh!'* of surprise, a faint wash of colour on her cheeks.

'Hi,' he greeted her, voice gruff, as she fumbled to turn off the radio.

'Hello.' Her smile was tentative and uncertain.

'I'm finished.' Her movements jerky, she continued gathering up her paintbrushes. 'What do you think?'

For the first time he dragged his disobedient gaze away from her and turned his attention to what had once been a square white boxroom, lacking warmth or character. What he saw rendered him speechless. The nursery had been transformed into something any young child would dream of, with an array of colourful cartoon characters dancing across the walls.

How had Holly achieved this? He turned a slow circle, finally arriving back to face her again, noting her nervousness as she clasped her hands together, her sky-blue eyes wide with uncertainty.

'You did this?' he managed, his tone betraying his incredulity.

'Y-yes.' She swallowed, her tongue-tip peeping out again to lick her lips. 'I'm sorry. Once I started I got a bit carried away. If you hate it I can paint over it. I—'

'Stop.' She did, nibbling the end of one finger with even white teeth. 'God, Holly, how did you manage it in so few days? I had no idea you had such a talent for art.'

Once more her cheeks flushed, giving her a becoming rosy glow. 'I haven't—not really. But I enjoyed it. I want Max to be happy.'

'Max will love it.' Still stunned at what she had done, he surveyed the room again, a lump in his throat. '*I* love it. It's the most incredible thing I've ever seen. Thank you.'

'It's my pleasure.'

An electric silence hummed between them and it took a tremendous effort of will for him to force himself to look away and not give in to the crazy urge to hug her. Instead, he crossed to the window, ostensibly to inspect the curtains— which, he discovered, she had made herself— but in truth it was a ruse to put distance between them.

'I didn't realise the time,' she murmured, sounding awkward again. 'I'd better go. If it's all right, I'll move my things in after breakfast tomorrow, ready for when Max comes home.'

Tomorrow. Everything was happening so fast. 'That's fine.' Which was a lie. It was far from fine. He needed to reinforce his barriers if he wasn't going to fall for her again.

As she jogged down the stairs and closed the

front door behind her he wondered what he'd agreed to. But whatever the cost to himself, Max needed Holly. He pressed the heel of one hand to his sternum, dismayed by the ache of yearning.

Would he never learn?

Despite everything, he was as vulnerable to Holly as he'd always been. For the sake of his son, and if his own heart wasn't to be trampled a second time, he had a few short hours to rebuild his defences before Holly moved in and turned his life upside down.

Again.

'Are you sure about this, Holly?'

As George parked the car outside Gus's house, Holly nodded in response to her friend's anxious query. Just as she had when Gina and Ruth expressed similar concerns, she hid her fears and doubts about the wisdom of her actions. She could see no other viable option: Max's needs overrode everything else.

Turning her head to hide her misgivings from George's probing gaze, Holly stared through the passenger window at Gus's solid semi-detached Victorian villa. Situated along a tree-lined road

in a quiet residential area of town, it was built of
sandstone with a slate roof—typical of the local
architecture—and there were views of the hills
from the master bedroom upstairs. A room she
didn't want to think about.

This house would be her home for the foreseeable future. A shiver ran down her spine. She'd
worked on the nursery for four consecutive days,
but she felt no less nervous at the prospect of ac-
tually *living* here. In what had been Julia's home.
Julia and Gus's *marital* home. Confined under
the same roof as Gus, the man who had chosen
her sister instead of her…the man who had broken her heart and who, despite everything, she
couldn't stop loving, foolish and hopeless though
that was.

She'd loved him from day one. Her body reacted the same way now as it had then. When
Gus looked at her through those incredible smoky
green eyes she had to force herself to remember
how to breathe, and his husky voice curled her
toes. An excellent doctor, he was warm, caring,
and gentle with patients. And, despite some of
her colleagues finding him reserved and distant

at first, she'd seen beyond the surface to the special man inside.

That he guarded his privacy was something she understood and respected. From that first day in August until the night of their ill-fated date-that-never-was they had been as close as it was possible to be without being physically intimate. But Holly's dream had shattered with Gus and Julia's betrayal, followed by the news of Julia's pregnancy, and then, in December, their hasty marriage. She'd been so hurt, so angry, so shocked... so jealous. January's escape from A&E had removed her from Gus's presence but had not removed Gus from her mind. Or her heart.

She enjoyed the Children's Ward, admired Sister Sharpe and welcomed working with George again, but resentment towards Gus and Julia remained. She felt she'd been forced from the dream job she'd loved and worked hard for. She missed Annie, Nathan, Will, Kelly, Gail, Carolyn and the others, who'd not just been colleagues, but friends, too. And she missed the cut and thrust of trauma nursing.

Since transferring, she'd had no contact with Gus until Wednesday's tragic events. Her emotions were in turmoil, and despite reassuring her friends otherwise she feared what lay ahead and was riddled with doubts.

'Holly?' George gave her a gentle nudge. 'You can change your mind, you know, and come home with me.'

Suppressing the urge to retreat to the sanctuary of the room she'd rented at George's, Holly shook her head. 'No. This is the right thing to do.'

'For whom?'

'For baby Max.' Holly shifted her attention from the imposing façade of the house and looked at George, whose grey eyes regarded her with unconcealed worry. Sighing, she made a further admission. 'And for Gus.'

What she didn't say was that it was also for herself. She knew she had fallen as madly in love with Max as she had with his father. She knew what dangerous ground she was on—which was why she'd hidden the true depth of her feelings from Gina, Ruth and George.

George's expression softened. 'Gus's determination to raise Max himself *is* admirable.'

Holly nodded. But then, she knew why this mattered so much to Gus. Abandoned hours after his birth, he knew nothing about his background or who his parents were. The thought of him growing up without any love or affection, passed from place to place like an unwanted parcel, still moved her to tears. His resolve that his son would grow up with the love, care and security he'd been denied was understandable.

'Time's a-wasting, George,' she said, with a light-heartedness she was far from feeling. 'Let's do this.'

Unable to delay the moment any longer, they climbed out of the car, and while George opened the hatchback and began unloading things Holly took a suitcase and went to the front door. She was deciding whether to use the key Gus had given her or ring the bell when the door opened and she was staring into deep green eyes—eyes that had the power to weaken her knees and turn her insides to mush.

As her gaze clashed with his and the familiar tingle of awareness percolated through her, tightening the aching knot deep inside her and setting her pulse racing, she wrestled with the dilemma that nagged more intensely with each day that passed.

How could she still feel so strongly for Gus after everything that had happened?

She didn't understand her emotions. She wished she felt nothing. Nothing but anger and hurt, still so raw, at what he had done. One look at Julia and Gus had been smitten, transferring his allegiance from her to her beautiful but selfish sister. Their closeness couldn't have meant anything to him. Not as it had to her.

A fresh wave of guilt assailed her. Julia had bullied her since childhood and done many unforgivable things. But now Julia was dead. Despite her friends claiming to understand her less than charitable feelings towards her sister, Holly felt bad. There was sorrow for the tragic loss of a young life, but her predominant emotions were hurt, anger and jealousy over Julia's final and worst betrayal…going after Gus. And succeeding. For which she blamed them both.

The betrayal touched her from the grave. Because what she could never forget and what continued to torture her was that, in the unlikely event of Gus ever looking at her again as he had when they first met, she would always know he'd chosen Julia instead. She'd always be second best. And, however much she might love him, she deserved more than that…more than Julia's leftovers.

Gus fought the desire that shot through him as he looked into Holly's sky-blue eyes. He was unable to read the changing emotions in them, but he sensed her reserve and momentarily panicked that she'd changed her mind about moving in. Because he needed her help with Max, he told himself, *not* because he craved her company.

Disconcerted, he stepped back to allow Holly inside, noticing the heavy suitcase she was carrying. 'Let me take that for you.'

'Thanks.' Her smile was hesitant as she handed him the case. 'I'll get another load.'

He watched as she turned and headed back down the path. The abundant hedge fronting the property hid his view of the car, but he had another view. A better view. And his disobedient gaze took full advantage, lingering on Holly's delicious curves, hugged by faded black jeans that emphasised the captivating wiggle of her bottom.

Cursing himself, he hurried upstairs and set the case on the bed in Holly's room. He'd offered her the master bedroom that had been Julia's domain but she'd declined, declaring herself satisfied with the smaller but well-proportioned third bedroom. As he slept in the second bedroom, Holly's decision meant that they were equally well-placed to attend to Max's needs as the nursery conveniently sat between them.

Heading back downstairs, he heard voices outside, followed by Holly's soft laugh. His footsteps slowed as a young woman around Holly's age stepped into the house. He'd seen her around the hospital wearing a staff-nurse uniform and, remembering his talks with Holly back in the days when they'd shared lunch breaks and confidences, he guessed this was George.

Georgia.

He smothered a laugh as he recalled how jealous and upset he'd been when he'd thought George was the man in Holly's life. This George—Holly's George—was definitely female! A couple of inches taller than Holly and a little less curvy, George had pretty elfin features, short, spiky chestnut hair and striking grey eyes. Her smile was broad and genuine, and she exuded energy and a natural friendly warmth.

Before either of them had the chance to speak, Holly returned to the porch and balanced the box she was carrying between her hip and the wall. 'Have you two never met?' she asked in surprise, looking from Gus to George and back again.

'No,' they answered in unison, sharing a smile.

'Gus, this is George Millar…George, meet Gus. He thought you were a man!' she added with an infectious giggle.

As Holly set down the box and headed back outside Gus struggled with his embarrassment. 'I'm sorry. I only thought that because of the name—certainly not seeing you,' he tried to explain, cursing his clumsiness and feeling foolish.

'No worries. It happens all the time!' George grinned, silver sparkles dancing in her eyes. 'I was christened Georgia, but everyone's called me George since I was a baby.' Smiling, she adjusted the bag she was carrying and held out her hand. 'It's good to meet you, Gus. I've heard so much about you.'

'That sounds ominous,' he responded as he shook her hand, her instinctive warmth helping him relax.

'Not at all. You're well-respected around the hospital.'

To say George's words shocked him was a major understatement. Respect had definitely not been in evidence when his colleagues—indeed, the whole hospital—had labelled him the villain for what had happened with Holly. And self-respect had been in even shorter supply with regard to his ill-judged night with Julia. For that he *had* been to blame. But despite shouldering the responsibility without protest, at least outwardly, he'd been annoyed and hurt that Holly's part in events had gone unquestioned and unacknowledged. In his mind it hadn't been as black and white as that.

He'd slowly won back the professional respect of his colleagues, but it appeared that Julia's death, the miraculous survival of Max, and staunch public support from Holly had completed his rehabilitation. He was grateful—yet a flicker of resentment remained.

George's smile faded, concern replacing the earlier humour. 'Gus, I'm so sorry for your loss.'

'Thank you.'

An awkward silence lingered, and Gus felt

guilty for accepting the kindness of someone who naturally assumed he was racked with grief and who knew nothing of the circumstances, or his shameful sense of relief. Picking up the box Holly had left in the porch, Gus led George upstairs.

'It's wonderful that Max is doing so well. Everyone is talking about your miracle baby,' George chattered as they reached Holly's bedroom and set down their respective loads. 'You must be so excited that he's coming home today.'

'I've been counting the hours,' he admitted with a smile.

George smiled back, a touch of mischief in her eyes. 'There's a good-natured competition brewing between us on the children's ward and your colleagues in A&E to claim babysitting rights!'

Gus pondered this, touched by the support. Aware that Holly could join them at any moment, he used the time alone with George to seek answers to some of his questions.

'You and Holly have been friends for a long time?' he asked, abandoning any pretence of subtlety.

'Over twenty years—since junior school,' she replied, chuckling at his exclamation of surprise.

'We trained together, which was fun—although this is the first time since we qualified that we've worked together. I went straight to Paediatrics while Holly chose A&E.'

He was eager to discover more, but the subject of their conversation arrived in the bedroom and his opportunity was lost. Holly looked wary at the sight of them talking together.

'Is there anything else to bring up?' Gus asked, regretting that his chance to question George had ended.

'I'm afraid so,' Holly confirmed ruefully.

George laughed. 'I don't know how we crammed it all in the car!'

'I'll go and make coffee—we have time before going to the hospital—then I'll bring up another load,' he offered, leaving them alone and returning downstairs.

With the coffee underway, Gus gathered up more of Holly's possessions from the diminishing pile stacked in the porch and started up the stairs. As he neared the top he heard the girls talking and, ashamed of himself for eavesdropping, let his steps falter.

'Are you going to be all right?' George queried with concern.

Holly's laugh was shaky. 'I hope so. If I re-member why I'm here,' she added, her enigmatic comment making him frown and wonder again about her motives—what lay behind her offer to help with Max?

'There's always a room for you at my house.'

'Thanks, George. But don't turn down any op-portunity to rent,' Holly insisted. 'If you get the chance for a new housemate or two, go for it.'

'There's no rush. Dad left me well provided for. I rent the rooms more for the company than for the money. I'll miss you, Holly. It's been fun having you around—like old times when we were kids!' Gus heard the waver in George's voice. 'It's going to seem even stranger when Kelly leaves for Australia in a couple of weeks. The cats and I will be rattling round the house on our own.'

'Kelly's really brave. I wonder what it would be like to nurse in a big city hospital like the one in Sydney?' Holly mused.

Gus's heart lurched at the thought of Holly leaving to take part in the exchange programme Strathlochan Hospital had organised with its counterpart in Australia, giving doctors and nurses the opportunity to swap places for a year.

'I wouldn't like it,' George admitted, and Holly laughed, the throaty sound tightening the ache in his chest.

'Given that you've rarely ventured as far from Strathlochan as Edinburgh,' she teased her friend, 'I can't imagine you popping off to Sydney!'

George joined in the laughter. 'Kelly's more adventurous than me.'

'And me. It's a wonderful opportunity, but I wouldn't do it,' she confided, and Gus's heart returned to a more normal rhythm. 'I hate to think of you in the house alone, though.'

'August will be the best time to find another housemate when the new intake descends on the hospital. That's weeks off, so you can come back if you need to.'

'Thanks, George, you've been fabulous. I don't know what I'd have done without you when I had to sell the house,' Holly confided, pain evident in her voice.

Gus remembered Holly telling him she'd had to sell her home due to her parents' wishes, but was there more to it? Hearing movement, and fearing

Holly and George would discover him lingering, he made a noise to alert them of his arrival, then continued up the stairs and into the bedroom.

The woman who continued to turn his life upside down looked round as he entered the room and he was struck by her natural beauty. He'd hoped Holly would be the mother of his children but she hadn't wanted him. Despite being a good nurse, Holly's total lack of interest in Julia's pregnancy had led him to expect a similar lack of interest in his son. The fierceness of her devotion to Max had completely bowled him over.

A sudden thought occurred to him …

What if Holly wanted custody of Max? Was *that* her motivation? If it was, she'd have the fight of her life. He would never give up his son. *Never.* The thought took root, nagging at him, reminding him to be cautious in the days ahead.

Holly moving in was far from ideal, given the tension between them, but Max was his paramount concern. Which meant getting used to Holly being around…and ignoring the way his heart turned over when he looked at her.

'Come down when you're ready and we can work out a schedule,' he suggested, backing out of the room and giving himself the chance to strengthen his protective shield.

Holly had slipped past his defences before and she'd let him down. It had been a bitter blow and one he'd never overcome. He'd failed to get her out of his system. She was dangerous, and he had to be careful not to leave himself open and vulnerable to her again. There were things that didn't make sense, and until he knew the truth he'd keep up his guard.

CHAPTER EIGHT

AFTER George's departure, Holly spent a few moments bringing order to her room and putting her toiletries in the space Gus had made for her in the shared bathroom. Before heading downstairs she stopped by the nursery, recalling Gus's surprise the night before when he'd seen the results of her efforts. His reaction had made the long hours she'd spent on the task worthwhile.

Since the previous night Gus had added finishing touches and organised the room. He'd even hung in the window the rainbow spinner she'd bought to entertain Max. An inbuilt mini solar panel absorbed the sunlight and turned the crystals hanging beneath, reflecting rainbows of colour around the room.

Excited by Max's imminent arrival home, she went down to the kitchen. Gus was sitting at the table, and she sensed a reserve in him that hadn't been there a short while ago. Maybe the act of her physically moving in had hit him as forcefully as it had hit her, slamming home the reality that they were confined under this roof together with Julia and the past hanging over them. Forbidden territory. But not forgotten…certainly not by her.

Would having Max at home make things easier? Holly hoped so. With any luck they'd be so focused on the baby's needs there wouldn't be time to notice the tension—or for her to brood over Gus, and what she'd lost. Once they returned to work their paths would only cross as they exchanged responsibility for Max. Or so she hoped. Again and again she repeated the mantra she'd used to reassure her friends…*she was doing the right thing for Max*. But doubts still nagged at her.

Gus looked up from the notepad on the table in front of him, his sultry green eyes guarded. 'Has George gone?'

'Yes. She had some errands to run.' Covering her nerves, Holly accepted the coffee he offered and sat down, keeping the solid width of the table between them. 'You've finished the nursery so well.'

'Its success is your doing, not mine.'

Although his gruff praise gave her a warm tingle, she was aware that her presence unsettled him. 'We've both done our part.' She sucked in a steadying breath and decided to tackle things head-on. 'Gus, I know this situation is far from how you planned it, and I know you don't really want me here, but this is about Max—not about us.'

'There is no *us*,' he pointed out, with a harshness that pierced her like a knife.

'No. I know that.' She knew it all too painfully, without the huge dose of salt being rubbed into a wound still deep and raw. Tears stung her eyes and she looked away, fighting against them and the emotions churning within. It was a struggle, but she regained control, although bitterness and sarcasm laced her words. 'I don't need reminding of the choice you made, Gus.'

'Holly…'

He fell silent, his frown deepening, and she watched as he dragged a hand through his hair, always a sure sign of his discomfort. Before he could say more, she pressed on. 'You mentioned a schedule?' she reminded him, steering them away from dangerous ground.

'Yes.' He appeared as keen as she was to keep things businesslike. 'Caring for a baby is new for us both.'

'We'll have much to learn, but once we establish a routine it will be easier. If we plan a rota for sharing the nights we should both get some sleep,' she suggested, pulling the pad and pen across the table and making some notes.

'What about your social life?'

A genuine laugh escaped her. 'What social life?'

'But—'

'Look, Gus.' She set down the pen and clenched her fingers together. 'This isn't something I've entered into lightly. My whole commitment is to Max.' Surely he knew her well enough to realise she'd never been a party girl? 'My time is accounted for with my shifts at the hospital, my friends and my study.'

'Study? What study?' he asked, looking genuinely perplexed.

'Didn't Julia tell you?' Her sister had no doubt told him a lot of other things, Holly reflected darkly. When Gus shook his head, she continued. 'I'm doing an Open University degree.'

A stunned silence followed before he spoke again, interest vying with confusion. 'I had no idea. A degree in what?'

'International Development, Environmental Studies and Geography.'

Gus sat back, stunned into silence. This was something else Holly had never shared with him, and he wondered why she'd kept it a secret when it was obviously important to her. It was one more question that remained unasked—for now. It was clear there were hidden depths to Holly…much he had yet to discover.

Frowning, he mulled over her earlier words, recalling the pain and accusation in her voice as she'd spoken them. *I don't need reminding of the choice you made, Gus.* What had she meant? *She* was the one who'd stood him up, rejecting him and his friendship, making a fool of him. What choice had he had with *her*? Self-disgust bit into him as he forced himself to acknowledge that Holly was not the only one to blame. He alone was responsible for his mistake with Julia.

As he wrestled with the inconsistencies, and all the things he didn't understand, Holly returned her attention to Max and suggested a workable rota.

'We also need to agree a fair amount for me to pay each week,' she said, once they'd sorted out sharing responsibilities for Max.

'Pay for what?' he asked, unsure where she was heading.

'My living expenses.' She shook her head as if exasperated with him. 'I don't expect you to support me, Gus. I intend to make a fair contribution to the household.'

Holly's attitude was the polar opposite of Julia's, and it took him a moment to gather his thoughts. 'But you're doing this to help. If I had to employ someone I'd have to pay them to live here, not the other way around,' he pointed out, seeing her bristle with indignation.

'I'm *not* someone else, and nor am I in your *employ*. Max is my flesh and blood. I most certainly do *not* want to be *paid* to care for him.'

'OK.' A sudden laugh bubbled out of him. She looked cute when she was angry! 'Why don't we let things settle and see how we go?'

The suggestion earned him a reluctant nod, but

her statement left him with little doubt he'd hear more on the subject in future.

'All right. For now.'

'Is there anything else?' he asked, glancing at his watch. The sooner he got to the hospital, the sooner he could bring Max home.

'There is something...'

After her spirited mood, she now sounded tentative and uncertain. The tension between them was making him cautious. 'What is it?'

'Gus, we can't change what happened in the past. Whatever we think of each other now, the most important thing is Max's well-being and ensuring he is thriving and loved.' She paused and turned her head, allowing him to see the sincerity and concern—but also the shadow of pain— in her amazing blue eyes. 'May I suggest we try to stop sniping at each other and keep our focus on Max?'

Whatever we think of each other now...

Holly's words rang in his head, disturbing him. What would she say if he asked her what she *did* think of him now? He was afraid to speculate. However, she was right. No matter how much the pain of the past nagged him, sarcastic comments and point-scoring served no purpose. And, however uneasy he was at the prospect of living closely with Holly, *his* needs and emotions were insignificant compared to his son's. For Max's sake he and Holly had to find an amicable way of living together.

'All right.'

His agreement was met with a wary, shy half-smile. 'Truce?' she ventured.

'Truce.'

Tentatively they shook hands, sealing the deal, but as he withdrew he felt disturbed by the instinctive reaction of his body to the touch of her silky-soft skin.

Pushing back her chair, Holly stood up, excitement and determination in her eyes. 'Let's bring Max home.'

Holly sat beside the cot in the moonlit nursery, a smile on her face as she watched Max sleeping. He was the most perfect baby. So beautiful. And he'd settled smoothly into his new environment and routine. Indeed, she allowed with a wry smile, he'd handled things with far greater equanimity than either she or Gus had managed!

A few days in and the rota they'd agreed was slowly being implemented. They hadn't taken much notice of it at first, as neither of them had been able to tear themselves away from Max. Even when one of them was officially off duty they lingered: not because they didn't trust the other—at least, not on *her* side, although she couldn't speak for Gus, who sometimes watched her with a frown on his face—but due to a genuine desire to be with the child and absorb every precious moment of his existence.

She'd taken to motherhood like a duck to water. The pain of yearning for what might have been continued to bite hard, but even without carrying the baby for nine months she'd bonded with Max from the first moment, when he'd been so small and bruised after his traumatic entry into the world. She found caring for Max to be instinctive, and was guided by him and by her own natural judgement. Both were thriving.

The most testing part for her was Gus. Sharing his house was fraught with difficulty. She was constantly on guard, trying to hide her jumbled feelings from him. But most troublesome was watching him blossom as a father. He'd adapted to his role with the same degree of delight and ease as she had to hers, and it was both an agony and a joy discovering a whole new side to him.

With Max, Gus let down his defensive wall and the real man she'd once glimpsed shone through, revealing so many aspects of his nature. He was funny, kind, caring, infinitely patient, warm and loving. It tore at her heart to see him interact with Max. She marvelled at the way his large hands gently cradled the fragile baby, protective, soothing and surprisingly dexterous when dealing with nappies or the fiddly fastenings on tiny clothes. Seeing the love in Gus's green eyes and witnessing Max's delight as his father tickled him or blew raspberries on his bare tummy melted her into a puddle.

But the wonder of those moments was countered by Gus's retreat when he looked at or spoke to *her*, as though he didn't trust her. It hurt. As did knowing that he was far beyond her reach. And in spite of everything she couldn't switch off her feelings for him. She was cross with him— and more so with herself for foolishly loving him. The pain intensified with each passing day.

Following their truce Gus had been civil, but

that somehow made her feel worse. The polite distance was so far removed from the closeness they'd shared before that it highlighted the chasm now between them.

Touching each other was proving to be unavoidable, which made her life so much more difficult. When she took Max from Gus it was impossible not to brush against him. She tried to keep contact to a minimum, because the lightest caress of skin against skin fired her blood and increased the terrible awareness that plagued her.

It was even worse when Gus inadvertently touched her. Every particle reacted and each nerve-ending tingled, her body screaming with the long-suppressed aching need. Earlier that evening, when Gus had scooped Max from her, his forearm had brushed across one of her breasts. Even now her flesh tingled in remembrance, and she hoped he hadn't noticed the immediate hardening of her nipple.

Soft music drifted through the house. Watching Max, Holly noticed how the sound soothed him: his mouth ceased the cute little movements it had been making. Satisfied all was well and Max was peaceful, she stifled a yawn and rose reluctantly to her feet. It was late, and having been up the night before she ought to take advantage of Gus being on baby-watch to get some much-needed sleep tonight.

Instead of returning to her room, however, she picked up her baby monitor—twin to the one Gus carried—and walked barefoot downstairs, drawn by the music. She halted on the threshold of the living room, surprised by the sight that greeted her. The patio door was open and Gus sat there, catching the soft breeze that relieved the sultry heat of the night. The music came not from the radio or a CD, as she'd anticipated, but from the saxophone Gus was playing. It was another new discovery. Intrigued, she listened, the hauntingly beautiful music bringing tears to her eyes.

Needing to be near him, she tiptoed closer, lost in the music, touched by the depth of melancholy that rang in each heart-wrenching note. The rawness ripped through her heart.

Gus must have sensed her presence because he turned his head, long lashes lifting, his green gaze clashing with hers as the note he was playing trailed into silence.

Holly hesitated.

So did Gus.

For several long moments time seemed suspended. Holly was aware of every rapid beat of her heart. An electric tension fizzed between them. Dressed only in her pyjama shorts and skimpy top, she crossed her arms in an effort to hide her body's response. As well as the aching knot that tightened low in her tummy, her nipples peaked against the soft cotton fabric of her pale blue camisole, wantonly craving his touch.

Finally, Gus spoke, his voice gruff. 'I'm sorry. I didn't mean to disturb you.'

'You didn't. It was too hot to sleep so I sat with Max for a while.' Her own voice wavered and dropped to a whisper. 'Please, don't stop playing.'

After an eternity, when she was sure he was going to refuse, Gus withdrew his enigmatic green gaze, picked up the sax and returned the mouthpiece to his lips. Once more the music called to her, pulling at her emotions, holding her in its thrall. It wasn't a piece she recognised but it spoke of loneliness, of loss, of intense inner pain.

'That was so beautiful,' she murmured hoarsely when the last note faded. 'What's it called?'

Something dark and sorrowful flashed in his eyes before he masked it. 'I haven't thought of a title yet.'

'*You* composed it?'

'Yes.'

Awed, she shook her head. 'That's amazing. You're so talented, Gus. Have you played professionally?'

'No.' He shrugged, looking self-conscious. 'I do it for me.' After a moment of hesitation he continued, an edge to his tone, the expression in his eyes unreadable. 'I didn't sit down with the intention of writing it. I was hurting, contemplating lost love, and the music flowed out of me with the emotion.'

He meant Julia. Holly winced with an all too familiar pain. Pain for Gus and his suffering. Pain for herself because he'd rejected her and loved another—and not just any other, but her sister.

'I'm sorry.'

Her broken words drew him closer and her heart nearly stopped as he cupped her face in his hands and brushed the tears from her cheeks with the pads of his thumbs.

'Don't cry for me,' he instructed huskily.

Her chest tightened as the breath locked in her lungs. Every fragment of her skin tingled. She couldn't look away, held captive by the intensity of his gaze, praying her need and love for him were not as glaringly obvious as they felt. Her legs felt too rubbery to support her much longer. All she wanted was lean into him, wrap her arms around him, hold and comfort him. And she wished with all her might that circumstances had been different…that he'd returned her feelings and chosen her over Julia.

What was he thinking? She could read nothing in his eyes. As his fingers stroked her face she bit her bottom lip to stop the trembling and silence, the moan of desire that sought freedom. After endless minutes when the tension had reached boiling point, she saw the shutters drop down, signifying his withdrawal and his emotional retreat. His hands fell away and he stepped back, leaving her feeling bereft and alone.

'You should be sleeping. I'll let you get to bed,' Gus suggested gruffly, turning his back to her as he took his time closing and locking the patio door.

Feeling the dismissal, the new rejection, Holly pressed the fingers of one hand to her mouth, stopping the protest and the plea from escaping. Instead, with tears stinging her eyes, she walked from the room and up the stairs. Moments later she lay on her bed, staring into the darkness. Her mind was full of Gus. She knew it would be a very long time before sleep came.

He'd hated every moment with Julia in his house, Gus admitted. They hadn't fitted on any level. It had been the first time he'd lived with anyone since he'd been a child, moving from one foster place to another and then the children's home. They'd not been happy experiences. He'd been the cuckoo in the nest, the one who didn't belong. Since then he'd been alone, so it had been a shock to the system when Julia had moved in. Having been alone most of his life, the loneliest he'd ever felt was being trapped in an unhappy marriage, living in the house with Julia, with a growing chasm separating them.

Consequently, he'd been nervous about Holly moving in. As days turned into weeks, however, he was discovering how very different sharing living space could be. For the first time the house felt like a home. He told himself it was because of Max, but he knew it wasn't true. Holly made the real difference. She'd added fresh flowers and scented candles, colourful throws and cushions—things he was not only surprised to notice but more amazed to find he enjoyed.

When not involved with Max, Holly kept to herself, studying towards the Open University exam she'd told him was in October.

'You never mentioned your degree to me before,' he'd pointed out, trying to understand why she'd kept so much back.

'I wasn't studying last year,' she'd explained, her gaze direct. 'I needed a break. But after Christmas I decided to continue—I need ninety more credits to gain the degree—so I enrolled for this course which started in February.'

The explanation had made sense, and he realised she'd not been excluding him. He'd enjoyed hearing about her degree. Indeed, he was alarmed by how much he enjoyed having Holly around, full stop—not just for her help with Max but for her companionship. He was on dangerous ground.

Holly was nothing like Julia. Julia had hoarded designer clothes, shoes and handbags. Holly's wardrobe contained casual jeans, shorts and tops alongside her uniforms. Plus a pair of colourful Wellington boots. The bathroom shelves were no longer overflowing. Holly's handful of items—deliciously scented shampoo and body lotion included, both of which he'd guiltily uncapped and sniffed—sat adjacent to his own.

Living with Holly was not only eye-opening but a real challenge to his determination to maintain his distance. Little by little she was burrowing back under his skin. And watching her with Max made things tougher. She was a natural mother and his son was thriving in her care.

The health visitor and GP with whom they kept regular appointments were delighted with Max's progress. Thankfully, there appeared to be no ongoing consequences from the alcohol Julia had consumed, nor from blood-loss and lack of oxygen after the accident. Max truly *was* a miracle—one he gave thanks for every day.

Caring for his son together, he and Holly had shared several poignant and funny moments… experiences that had not only brought them both closer to Max but closer to each other, too. Discovering that Holly was keeping a baby diary—recording information about Max from the moment of his birth, including photographs, hand and footprints, and even a lock of his hair— had surprised and delighted him.

They had dissolved into uncontrollable giggles at some of the comical faces Max pulled. And he recalled one time when he'd lingered, unable to leave Max, watching Holly change his nappy with a strange look on her face.

'What's wrong?' he'd asked as she'd fidgeted and wrinkled her nose.

She'd shaken her head and huffed out a laugh. 'My nose itches!'

He'd chuckled, seeing her predicament as her hands were fully occupied. 'Let me help you.' Without thinking, he'd leaned over, reached out a couple of fingers and gently rubbed the tip of her nose. 'Here?'

'Y-Yes.'

Her voice had caught and he'd looked up, his gaze locking with hers. Awareness and confusion had mingled in sky-blue eyes. The temptation to kiss her had been so overwhelming he wasn't sure what he would have done had Holly not stepped back, breaking the contact. Electric tension had throbbed in the air between them.

The night she'd found him playing the sax also remained imprinted on his mind. Julia had hated his music. That Holly had been moved was obvious, and he'd come so close to confessing he'd written the piece for her. Instead he'd lied, claiming it was untitled. It wasn't. He'd named it the moment it had formed in his mind: *Holly's Lament.* She was the only woman he'd ever loved and her rejection was a painful wound that was nowhere near close to healing. Self-preservation led him to keep the barrier between them, but it was increasingly difficult to remember why he had to keep her at a distance.

Today had been his first day back at work and he'd missed Max—and Holly—terribly. She'd returned to the hospital a few days ago and they were adjusting to the new routine. He'd been assigned to Minors again, the senior consultant on duty having suggested he ease back in after a month away. Given how rusty he felt, it had been the right decision.

His hours at work had seemed far longer than

usual now that he had a baby son waiting for him. As soon as he entered the house, his tension began seeping away. Hearing noises in the kitchen, he tossed his new car keys into a bowl on the table at the foot of the stairs and walked down the hall, enjoying the warm, welcoming feel of home.

Tired and hungry, all he wanted was to see Max.

And Holly, who continued to arouse confusing emotions inside him, setting his head and his heart at war.

'Hi. Everything OK?'

'Fine. Max has been good as gold,' Holly smiled in response to Gus's question as he strode into the kitchen.

The hours without him had seemed horribly long, and her pulse raced as she drank in the sight of him. Dressed in a grey T-shirt, and faded jeans that lovingly hugged his long legs, he was the epitome of male gorgeousness and she cursed her wayward heart and disobedient body for their instant reactions to him. Gus continued to draw her like a moth to a flame…a moth that had been singed on numerous occasions but still succumbed to the lure, however dangerous.

'How was it back in A&E?' she asked, distracting herself.

'Tiring. And good. But long.'

Holly nodded in understanding. His words mirrored her feelings when she'd had to leave Max and go to work. She listened as Gus described some of the cases he'd seen in Minors, from a precocious toddler with a bead stuck in her ear to a middle-aged man who'd fired a nail gun through his foot while installing decking.

Holly looked up from preparing a salad and watched Max wave his fist towards Gus. The gesture and his gurgle of pleasure as his father gently caught his little hand and kissed it brought a lump to her throat and an ache of longing inside her.

'He missed you,' she told him, declining to add that Max hadn't been the only one.

Gus plucked the baby from the Moses basket and nuzzled Max's chubby cheeks. 'Me, too,' he admitted huskily, flicking a brief but intense gaze in her direction.

She turned away from the sight of father and

son lovingly interacting with each other and put the finishing touches to the salad, which would accompany the quiche she'd made for supper. Putting the bowl in the fridge, she reflected on how, in a few short weeks, Max had become the centre of her life. So much so that she'd been doing a great deal of soul-searching and now realised she needed to talk to Gus. She glanced at him nervously, unsure how he would react to her suggestions.

Gus closed the gap between them, coming near enough for her to enjoy his familiar aroma: clean warm man mixed with the subtle, earthy musk of his aftershave. A heady, sexy combination. As he handed her a drowsy Max their hands touched and Gus's arm brushed against her, sending a shiver of awareness zinging along her nerve-endings. Disconcerted, she took a step back, her gaze meeting his.

She could feel each rapid beat of her heart as he reached out a hand and tucked a stray wisp of hair behind her ear. Her skin tingled. He lingered for several seconds before slowly withdrawing, allowing his fingertips to whisper a caress against her cheek. The tension was electric, humming between them with a conflicting mix of awkwardness and intimacy. It was only when Gus moved to take a can of cola from the fridge that she was released from his spell.

Unsettled by her complicated, dangerous feelings for Gus, Holly hugged Max and buried her face against him, breathing in his sweet baby scent. As Gus leant against the counter, taking a long pull of his drink, she exhaled a shaky breath and plucked up the courage to broach the subject preying on her mind.

'Can we talk?' she asked.

'All right.' Looking wary, Gus ran the fingers of one hand through his hair, leaving it attractively mussed. 'What about?'

Having won his cautious acceptance, she cleared her throat, trying to inject more steadiness into her voice. 'I want to make some changes to our agreement.'

Sultry green eyes studied her with an intensity that stole her breath. Every part of her felt alive. Moving to sit at the table, she adjusted Max in her arms, rubbing her cheek against the fuzz of soft brown hair on his head. Anxious and uncertain, she waited for Gus's reaction.

CHAPTER NINE

'CHANGES?' Anxiety twisted inside him at Holly's request. As he watched her cuddle Max, a sudden fear gripped him. Was he was going to lose her? Did she want to leave? He sat down opposite her and asked the all-important question. 'What kind of changes?'

'How would you feel if I cut back my hours?'

For a second his heart almost stopped. 'Your hours here with Max?'

'No!' She frowned, carefully adjusting Max, who had fallen asleep in her arms. 'My work hours at the hospital. It'll mean I bring in less money to contribute to the expenses,' she hurried on, before he could express the relief rushing through him, 'but time with Max is precious—especially in these early weeks and months when he's changing and growing so quickly. I don't want to miss anything.'

'I've told you I don't expect you to pay house-hold bills, so that isn't a problem,' he reassured her.

'Yes, but—'

He held up a hand, silencing her as she tried to rush on before he'd finished speaking. 'You want to know how I'd feel if you stayed home more with Max?'

'Yes,' she whispered, sky-blue eyes wide with worry.

'Envious.' He smiled as Holly blinked at him in surprise. 'So often these last few weeks I've wished I could be with Max all the time. Returning to work today was *so* hard. I be-grudged every second away from him,' he con-tinued, not adding that he'd missed her almost as much as his son. 'The department is so well-run, the team so good, I doubt they'd notice if I wasn't there!'

'Of course they'd notice. More importantly, so would your patients,' she added, a huskiness edg-ing her words.

Her compliment warmed him. 'Thanks for the vote of confidence. Still, I'd give up work in an instant to—'

'Gus, you can't!' Holly's shocked exclamation

interrupted him. 'You have a vital year of completing your specialist training, including a rotation in Intensive Care. I know Max is a priority, but your career is important, too—for *both* your futures,' she stated, with a passion that brought a lump to his throat.

'Your support means a lot,' he told her honestly, intrigued as her cheeks bloomed with delicate colour. 'Isn't *your* career important?'

'Yes, but I can take a break without losing ground.'

Holly paused, tucking a wisp of hair behind her ear, reminding him that in a moment of weakness he'd done the same thing minutes before. His fingers still tingled from the forbidden feel of her peach-soft skin.

'I love my job,' she continued, 'and I'll always need to keep updated, but as a senior staff nurse I'm at the level I want to be for the foreseeable future. Moving up a grade means more administration and less hands-on time with patients.'

'And caring for patients is what means the most to you,' he added, knowing what an excellent nurse she was.

She nodded, amusing him as her cheeks pinkened further. 'Yes.'

'I understand. And what I was going to say before you interrupted me,' he teased gently, 'is that you have my backing. Max will only benefit from more time with you.'

'Thanks, Gus.'

He met Holly's gaze, relieved to see an absence of the shadows that too often dimmed the light in her captivating blue eyes. A shy, natural smile curved her lips and a wave of desire swelled inside him. Despite her public rejection, he still responded to Holly as instinctively as the day they'd met.

On the night that had irrevocably changed his life he'd allowed his bitter disappointment and hurt to affect his judgement. It had been easier to blame Holly and find fault rather than accept that she simply hadn't returned his feelings. Looking at his son, cradled lovingly in Holly's arms, he gave thanks for his beautiful, special baby. However unplanned and unexpected, whatever sacrifices he'd made, he could *never* regret Max.

The awkwardness between Holly and himself had eased and, however temporarily, they'd slipped back into the easy camaraderie they'd shared in the beginning. It brought home how much he'd missed her…her friendship, her smile, her humour, her kindness. He'd been a fool to believe he'd got over her in the last few months. He hadn't. But he had no idea what—if anything—to do about it. Because if he put his heart on the line again and she rejected him a second time, he didn't think he'd recover.

He had to keep his focus fixed on Max's needs, which meant masking his feelings for Holly. She'd committed herself even more fully to Max. How would she react to his plan to safeguard his son's future?

'I have something to discuss, too,' he began, watching as she softly brushed her cheek against Max's downy head.

An edge of wariness returned, dimming her smile. 'What is it?'

'We've seen how precious life is…and how precarious. It can be snatched away when we least expect it,' he began, with a mix of emotions, predominantly guilt, assailing him as he thought of

Julia. 'I want to put a legal framework in place to protect Max—in case the worst should happen.'

He saw Holly shiver. 'It's horrible to think about, but it's the right thing for Max. What have you in mind?' she asked, a waver in her voice.

'My idea is twofold.' Crossing his arms, he leaned on the table. 'First I want to legalise your guardianship of Max to ensure you're both protected if something happens to me.'

'Gus, don't,' she implored, her voice throaty with emotion, long dusky lashes slowly lifting to reveal the tears shimmering in her eyes.

She reached a hand across the table and he acted instinctively, one of his hands covering hers in a gesture of understanding and comfort. At once his body responded to the touch of her soft skin and the feel of her small hand enveloped in his.

'Don't worry, I'm not planning on going anywhere,' he told her, trying to lighten the atmosphere.

Dared he imagine from her distress that Holly might care for him after all? Or was he fooling himself again? Most likely it was a natural response after what had happened to Julia rather than concern for him.

'I also want to appoint godparents. Should the worst happen, I want Max to have people we trust in his life,' he continued, focusing his mind back on his plans.

'That makes sense,' she agreed, withdrawing her hand and cuddling Max closer. 'Anyone in mind?'

Missing her touch, he refolded his arms, a frown knotting his brow. He wasn't the most social of people, and whilst he now enjoyed a good working relationship with his colleagues he couldn't say he'd ever had any real friends. Apart from Holly. But making a decision on where to place his trust regarding the care of his son had been relatively easy.

'Given the role he played in saving Max's life, I'd like to ask Frazer.' Memories of that terrible day brought a fresh edge of emotion to his voice. 'With his and Callie's first baby overdue and arriving any minute now they'll be experiencing parenthood with a child of a similar age.'

As Max stirred in her arms and yawned, blowing a cute little bubble in the process, Holly smiled, gently wiping his mouth and chin as she soothed the baby with the kind of natural care Gus had come to expect. 'Frazer and Callie would be perfect.'

'OK.' Finishing his can of cola, he pulled a pad and pen towards him and jotted down some notes. 'Because of their support and your close-ness with them I'd like to ask Seb and Gina, too. Is that all right?'

Rocking Max gently, Holly looked up, and Gus saw the suggestion of fresh tears in her eyes. 'More than all right. Are you sure?'

'Very sure.'

A smile rewarded him and brought a radiant bloom to her face. 'Thank you.'

It was a small thing he could do to please her, yet he felt a warm glow—and a massive sense of relief—that after doing the wrong things so often in the past he had finally done something right.

'I'll ask Frazer, Callie, Seb and Gina if they're willing to do it.' He cleared his throat to banish the roughness of emotion. 'We have an appoint-ment with the solicitor next week about Julia's estate, so we can discuss how to do things then. Is that OK?'

'Fine.'

He was thankful they were in agreement, but disappointed that the mention of Julia had changed the atmosphere and increased the tension again. As Holly whisked Max away to change his nappy Gus rose to his feet and began to set the table for supper. Mentioning Julia made him realise how much she still stood between Holly and himself. She'd told him some unfavourable things about Holly and had hinted at others—things he hadn't wanted to believe but which, he was ashamed to admit, he had used to persuade himself he was better off without Holly.

Now, thanks to Max, he was rediscovering Holly all over again—and one by one he was questioning the things Julia had said. In the weeks since Holly had moved in they'd taken the first cautious steps on the route back to friendship, but it would be all too easy to stuff things up again.

There were so many questions he wanted to ask Holly—so many answers he needed about the past, about what had gone wrong. But it never seemed like the right time to raise them. Until they resolved old issues there could be scant hope of winning back lost ground. He would have to tread slowly and carefully. Where his feelings would lead him, and whether Holly could ever come to see him as anything other than Max's father, Gus didn't know. Only time would tell.

They swiftly settled into the new routine. When she'd first moved in, Holly reflected, both she and Gus had gone out of their way to be polite and observe their new-found truce. But as the days and weeks had passed some of the easy camaraderie and closeness they had enjoyed when they'd first met had returned.

A different kind of tension had taken over. An electric tension. An unmistakable and all too familiar awareness. One that simmered beneath the surface, pooling like the lava lake of a volcano, waiting for the moment when the pressure became too great and it erupted in spectacular fashion. It was a prospect that both scared and excited her.

Having secured Gus's agreement to cut back her work hours, Holly had wasted no time putting her plan into action. The hospital's administration had been supportive. As had Erica Sharpe.

Holly recalled the day she'd taken Max to the hospital to show him off to the Paediatric staff who'd cared for him so well in the first days of his life. Before meeting Gus in A&E at the end of his shift, she'd stopped by the Children's Ward.

'I can see why you're captivated,' Erica had admitted, showing her soft side as she'd cooed over Max. 'He is the most beautiful baby.'

Holly's heart had filled to overflowing with love and pride. 'He has good genes. His mother was beautiful.' She kept to herself how gorgeous she found Max's father.

'A manufactured kind of beauty though it was.' The sharp remark was typically Erica, and Holly had hidden a guilty smile. 'One shouldn't speak ill of the dead,' the buxom sister had continued, 'but thank goodness Max doesn't appear to have inherited his mother's temperament. He's wonderfully serene and equable.'

'Yes, he is.' A fresh spear of guilt had pierced her as she'd agreed with her superior. She would have liked to believe motherhood would change Julia, but…

'I'm worried you're setting yourself up for heartbreak, Holly. It's no secret you had feelings for Gus at one time. And now you're so attached to Max…' Erica had spoken bluntly, making Holly blush and give thanks that Erica had no idea her feelings for Gus persisted.

Although concern and kindness had softened the older woman's voice, Holly had frowned. 'I don't understand.'

'I know you, my dear. Everything that makes you such a special person and a wonderful nurse will, I fear, make life very hard for you.'

'What do you mean?' she'd asked, a ripple of unease assailing her as her formidable advisor issued the words of caution.

With a sad smile, Erica had shaken her head. 'However much you may wish it, Holly, you're *not* Max's mother. Gus is a young, attractive man, and one day he's likely to remarry. Where will that leave you?'

Even now Erica's comments sent icy chills down Holly's spine. Max had captured her heart the second she'd seen him. And the idea that she might one day have to stand by and again watch Gus fall in love with someone else filled her with pain and dread. Erica had no idea her warnings came too late. Holly was in too deep to save herself. Handing Max, and his father, over to some other woman was a nightmare too horrific to consider.

Disturbed, Holly forced herself to think of other things. Happy things. Like new arrivals. After keeping everyone waiting for eight days, Callie had finally given birth to a beautiful baby girl called Isobel. Frazer had taken to fatherhood with the same panache as Gus, and he'd followed through on his intention to give up flying once the baby arrived. Having qualified as a consultant, and with a vacancy open in Strathlochan's A&E department, he would soon move from the air ambulance to the hospital. Holly was thankful he'd been a flight doctor when Max had so desperately needed his skills.

As the sun continued to shine through August she and Max spent time with Callie and Izzy— and Frazer's Border terrier Hamish—taking walks in the park, by the loch, or in the castle grounds. She and Callie enjoyed comparing notes on caring for their charges. And, with the two babies bonding, there had been much teasing that in twenty years' time they'd be planning Max and Izzy's wedding!

Holly's smile faded as her thoughts turned from happy arrivals to sad goodbyes. Kelly had set off for her year nursing in Australia on the exchange programme, and despite the promise of regular e-mail contact between Strathlochan and Sydney she would be missed. Holly worried about George, rattling round the big old house on her own with only the cats for company. She hoped that at least one of the new intake of young doctors and trainee nurses descending on Strathlochan throughout the month would become a good housemate for George.

And, hardest of all, before August ended Ruth would leave to embrace her new life with Rico in Florence. Holly knew Gina was as delighted as she was to see Ruth so happy and cherished by Rico, but she also knew tears would be inevitable when departure day arrived.

Rico and Seb were cousins, and very close, so Holly was consoled by the knowledge that they would all see each other as often as possible. Invitations to Florence and Elba remained open, and Ruth was keeping her home in Strathlochan for holidays and weekends.

It was at Ruth's cottage on the outskirts of town

that she and Max had spent an afternoon picking
an abundance of soft fruit—unfortunately without Ruth, who'd been working out her last days
as a GP at the town's biggest doctors' surgery.

'I hate to think of my fruit and vegetables
going to waste,' Ruth had remarked when Holly
and Gina had seen her the previous weekend.
'Promise to help yourselves to whatever you can
use.'

At home in the kitchen, with the back door open
to let in the late afternoon breeze and the sound
of the gently tinkling windchime hanging outside, Holly glanced at Max, asleep in his Moses
basket. Smiling, she began the task of sorting
out her bounty of berries and currants. As she
worked, deciding which to freeze and which to
make into jam, setting aside the ones that needed
to be eaten straight away, her thoughts turned to
the christening and to the visit she and Gus had
made to the solicitor.

Frazer, Callie, Seb and Gina had all enthu-
siastically accepted being godparents, and arrangements for a quiet ceremony were in hand.
As was the paperwork to deal with legal guardianship. When Gus had first mentioned it Holly

hadn't been unduly fussed, but in the light of Erica Sharpe's cautionary words safeguarding her rights with Max had become an urgent priority.

The bad news was that the solicitor—who'd handled legal matters for her family for as long as Holly could remember—had revealed the true situation relating to Julia's estate.

'Our searches have found no evidence of a will,' James Russell had explained, and although disappointed Holly hadn't been surprised to learn of Julia's failure to make preparations.

Frowning, Gus had sat forward attentively. 'Do her assets go to the government?'

'No. As her legal next of kin—and because she was not declared without life until after his birth,' the solicitor had informed them, 'Max is sole beneficiary.'

'Thank God,' Gus had responded, pleasing her, as it suggested his thoughts—like hers—were on Max.

The kindly, balding sixty-year-old had opened the file in front of him. 'I have to warn you… Julia's finances are a mess. We've been through all the paperwork and there's no easy way to say it. Apart from any items of value you have of hers at home—jewellery, for example—Julia *has* no assets.'

'That can't be right.' Holly remembered whispering the words. She'd been so shocked that for once she'd scarcely been aware of Gus.

'I'm sorry, Holly.' James's smile had been grave and apologetic. 'There's nothing left.'

The extent of Julia's debts shouldn't have come as such a surprise. Holly pressed a clenched fist to her aching chest as she contemplated again the ramifications of all James had told them. Julia had promised never to get into debt again and to get help for her self-confessed gambling problem. Those had been the conditions under which Holly had given Julia money and bailed her out of serious trouble. The agreement had been concluded in James's office, but Julia hadn't meant any of it. Something she had gleefully made clear later. There would be no savings account into which she would make deposits when she was back on her feet, and Holly would not be repaid.

Holly wasn't bothered that she'd never see a penny of the money herself. She'd lived without it up to now and would continue to manage. What pained her was the fact that the inheritance that should have provided for Max's future had been squandered by Julia with such selfish disregard.

She'd been grateful that James, the soul of discretion, had told Gus nothing of past events or of her own role in them. She didn't doubt that Gus had questions, but thankfully they'd remained unasked…so far. She had no wish to reveal the details to him, wanting to protect his memories of the woman for whom he grieved. And so Julia continued to be a ghostly spectre between them.

Succumbing to temptation, Holly popped a raspberry into her mouth, wishing the tangy burst of flavour would take away the sour taste left by her thoughts. Whether it helped or not she couldn't say: her attention was diverted by the sound of the front door closing, followed by footsteps treading down the hallway.

Gus was home.

Her heart gave its customary flutter and her breath hitched, her pulse racing at the prospect of seeing him. Masking her emotions, she turned as he entered the room and smiled.

'Hello,' she greeted, basking in the sight of him.

'Hi. Have you two had a good day?'

'Lovely.' And it was even better now he was home. Not that she could tell him that. She watched out of the corner of her eye as he crossed to the Moses basket where Max was waking from his nap. 'He heard your voice.'

Pleasure lit Gus's face. 'Did you wake up for your papa, half-pint?'

Max had received his first set of immunisations at eight weeks, when the GP had pronounced himself delighted with the progress made, reminding Holly of Gus's unwavering insistence that Max had entered the world four weeks early.

'He's changing and developing every day,' she commented as Gus picked Max up and cuddled him.

'He certainly is. I never tire of seeing his smile.'

Gus looked at her, and as their eyes met they shared a moment of intimacy. 'I know.' She struggled to bring her shaky voice under control. 'He's responding so much—copying expressions and gurgling back when you or I speak to him,' she added, glowing with pride at his growing achievements. And he was so handsome... just like his father.

'Have his eyes changed colour?' Gus asked, studying his son's face.

'Definitely.' She'd noticed the difference, too. 'They're more denim-blue.'

Max had lost the newborn look and was gaining more control of his movements, reaching out and trying to grasp things, beginning to suck his fist and thumb. He was lively and interested, and loved being read to and listening to music—especially when Gus played the sax. He'd been sleeping through for some time, allowing them undisturbed nights, and as his character continued to emerge his sweet nature remained. He was easygoing, and his sense of fun delighted her.

Gus was talking softly to Max, who gurgled in response. Seeing father and son together always stole her heart. Gus was so loving—gentle yet strong—and so protective. Holly returned to her task, wishing this scene they re-enacted daily was real…that they were a proper family and that she was not only Max's true mother but Gus's wife, too. It was a hopeless fantasy, but that didn't stop her dreaming.

She was startled when Gus moved to her side, Max cradled in one arm, brushing against her.

The touch of his skin set hers aflame. He leaned in and pinched a couple of raspberries from her bowl.

'Hey!' she admonished, insanely breathless from his nearness.

Gus popped the ripe fruit into his mouth, his chuckle and rare cheeky grin nearly seizing her lungs. 'You *have* been busy. Is this the result of your raid on Ruth's garden?'

'Yes. Max and I had a lovely afternoon and the freezer is stuffed with fruit. We'll be eating pies and crumbles for months! I'm going to make jam, too,' she told him, chattering like a flustered schoolgirl.

'I'm not complaining!'

Distracted by her awareness of his close proximity, she was slow to react when he selected another raspberry and slid it into her mouth. The pad of his thumb caught on the plump fullness of her lower lip.

Holly froze.

The air felt alive, crackling with electricity. Her gaze locked with his. As the berry burst and filled her mouth with its tangy richness she couldn't help but swallow and lick her lips. Gus's smoky eyes darkened. Holly could hear every rapid beat of her heart.

For one insane moment she thought he was going to kiss her. She tensed and drew away, desperate not to betray how intensely she craved for him to do just that. At once Gus stepped back and withdrew his gaze, breaking the magnetic spell between them. While she wrestled with her disappointment, and her fear that she had somehow exposed her feelings, he returned his attention to Max, cuddling his son close and kissing his soft cheek.

'Has he had his bottle?' Gus asked, with no sign of the previous fun or intimacy remaining in his voice.

'Not yet.' Fingers shaking, she tightened her grip on the bowl. 'It's ready. I thought you'd like to feed him if you were home in time.'

'Thanks.'

Gus sat at the table to feed Max, and although he was focused on his son, and relishing time with him after a long shift at work, he was aware of Holly, too.

What must she think of him? She'd withdrawn

so quickly she must have sensed his desire to kiss her. He smothered a groan. What had possessed him to let down his guard? She'd smelled of sunshine, summer berries and something uniquely Holly…feminine, warm and arousing. He should never have fed her that raspberry. It had seemed a simple gesture—a natural part of the humour they'd shared—but he'd overstepped the mark, allowing the attraction, the needing, the wanting, to show itself.

He watched as Holly took the local newspaper from the table and shooed an inquisitive wasp away from the fruit, ushering it out of the open back door. As she returned to her tasks he reflected on how natural she was in this domestic setting. Spending more time at home with Max agreed with her. And it wasn't just Max who felt the benefit, Gus allowed…his stomach approved, too.

'Have you always enjoyed cooking?' he asked as she mixed a crumble topping, covered the fruit and put the dish in the oven.

'I loved helping Mum on baking days as a child.' She glanced at him, her smile reminiscent. 'She was a wonderful cook. "Plain home food", she called it, nothing fancy, but it was delicious. She made her own bread, and we had all sorts of cakes, biscuits and puddings to come home to. It's nice having a chance to feed others.'

The aromas permeating the kitchen made his tummy rumble. 'You have a grateful recipient of your food here.'

'Thanks.' A flush of pleasure brought a rosy glow to her cheeks.

As Max enjoyed his bottle, Gus reflected on their visit to the solicitor. He'd been shocked to discover how desperate Julia's financial situation had been—something she'd lied about—but how that had affected Holly he wasn't sure. Given the way James Russell had consoled her, and Holly's pale cheeks and shocked expression, something was wrong. But what? He was wary of upsetting the truce between them by asking questions and raising contentious issues.

One task he'd been putting off was sorting Julia's belongings. It wasn't a prospect he relished, but it needed to be done. And he had to find out what Holly wanted to keep, and what her views were on disposing of the rest.

As Max finished his milk Gus shifted him to

his shoulder and gently patted his back to wind him. A surprisingly loud and satisfied belch emerged and Gus looked up, meeting Holly's amused gaze.

'My son...the champion burper,' he commented wryly, and she laughed, the infectious sound warming him.

'Make the most of it, Maxie,' she advised with a grin. 'This is the only time in your life that you'll be encouraged to burp like that and be praised for doing it!'

Sharing the laughter, Gus cuddled Max close, grateful that following his abrupt entry into the world his son was now the picture of health. Max was growing so quickly, and Holly was right about the way he changed and developed every day.

Much of Max's happy contentment and sunny disposition were due, Gus believed, to Holly's loving care. He wished she was Max's real mother. The admission hit him hard. Time with Holly had given him a taste of what might have been had things been different. Had Holly returned his feelings and not stood him up and rejected him. Had he not made the terrible error with Julia. Self-disgust and deep regret filled him. If only things had been different and this tableau of a happy family was true. He wanted to believe that Julia would have loved their son, but he doubted she would ever have adapted so readily to the day-to-day hands-on role that came so naturally to Holly.

With his thoughts back on Julia, Gus cleared his throat and broached the difficult task ahead of him.

'I think it's time I started sorting out Julia's things,' he told Holly, who leaned back against the counter, facing him.

'OK.' She lowered long dusky lashes, masking her expression. 'I'm sorry. I know it's not a nice thing to do. Do you want some help?'

'Thank you, no. Not to begin with, at least.' He appreciated her offer, but he'd heard her reluctance and didn't want to subject her to more pain than necessary. 'Is there anything you'd like to keep?'

She frowned and shook her head. 'I don't think so.'

'What about clothes? There are lots of designer things in the wardrobes,' he remarked, puzzled by her humourless laugh. 'Can't you make use of any of them?'

'Hardly! Julia was elegant and fashionable, not to mention incredibly slender—unlike me. I'm a jeans and T-shirt girl. Even if I were more stylish I'd never fit into her clothes,' she added with a rueful smile.

Her comments were made without edge or envy. She really believed what she was saying, Gus realised with shock. With her soft curves and natural beauty Holly was vastly more feminine and appealing than Julia had been—but he could hardly say that without revealing how he felt about her. He wanted more than anything to tell her, but doing so would mean confessing that he was a fraud—that his marriage had been a sham and he wasn't grieving as Holly and everyone else believed. It was a dilemma of his own making, and as he wrestled with it Holly diverted his attention.

'There is one thing I'd like to have...'

'Go on,' he invited, intrigued.

She clasped her hands so tightly that her knuckles whitened. 'Julia took the family photograph album. I don't know if it's here, but—'

'If I find it I'll make sure you get it,' he promised as her words trailed off. He could hear how much it meant to her, though it was a small enough request.

'Thank you.' Her relief was obvious as her shoulders relaxed and she unclasped her hands. 'There's something else, Gus.' She hesitated and he waited, curious to learn what was on her mind. 'I was just thinking… It would be good if you put some things aside for Max. It doesn't have to be much, but a memory box of things he can have when he grows older to remember his mother.'

A lump lodged in Gus's throat. He was touched by Holly's generous suggestion. He knew the sisters had been at odds, yet Holly's only thought was for Max and preserving good memories of the mother the boy would never know. It was another example of why his son was so lucky to have Holly in his life.

'That's a lovely idea. Thank you.'

She nodded, looking shyly embarrassed. Standing up, he returned Max to his Moses basket, smiling as his son stretched his limbs before giving a big yawn. He would never tire of watching him.

'Are you hungry?'

'Starving,' he confirmed in response to Holly's question, dragging his gaze from Max and turning to face her. 'Things were so busy today none of us got a break for a proper meal.'

'Don't tell me…you got through the day on endless mugs of tea and raiding the vending machine for chocolate?' she teased him.

'Guilty as charged.'

Shaking her head, she tried unsuccessfully to look cross. 'There's salad in the fridge. And I made a quiche earlier.'

'Plus the crumble in the oven. With ice cream?' he added hopefully, making her laugh again.

'Maybe!'

He rubbed his stomach in anticipation. 'Have I time to change?'

'Plenty.'

'I'll be down in a few minutes,' he promised.

Leaving the kitchen, Gus jogged upstairs and, after a quick wash in the bathroom, went to his bedroom to change into jeans and a T-shirt. Eager to sample the food awaiting him, he was just leaving his room when Max, who rarely even cried, began screaming at the top of his lungs.

The sound ripped Gus to shreds and brought a chill to his spine.

What the hell had happened?

CHAPTER TEN

'Gus? Oh, dear God! *Gus*!'

Holly's frantic call galvanised him into action and he rushed downstairs to the kitchen. 'What's wrong?'

Tears were streaming down Holly's cheeks as she hugged Max close. 'He's been stung by a wasp. I didn't see anything at first—he just started screaming. Then I found it inside the corner of his mouth. I got it out straight away—it's dead—but it must have stung him at least once on the tongue or in the mouth. The swelling began immediately,' she told him brokenly, pushing the back door shut with her foot.

Gus's heart nearly stopped as he saw how quickly the swelling was spreading over Max's face, mouth and throat. He wanted to grab his son, to hold him, comfort him, protect him, but every second counted and they needed to get to the hospital.

'Take Max to the car, Holly,' he instructed, reaching for his mobile phone. 'I'll ring A&E.'

Although his words were calm, he felt panicked inside. His heart was pounding. Fear threatened to paralyse him. But he had to function to help his son. Running down the path to his car, he phoned his colleagues to forewarn them of their arrival, then scrambled behind the wheel.

As a tearful Holly tried to soothe Max, whose distressed cries only added to his difficulty breathing, Gus drove to the hospital, praying they'd arrive in time to prevent a minor stupid incident taking his precious miracle baby away from him.

'Holly, give Max to me.'

Meeting them at the emergency doors, after what seemed the longest journey of her life, registrar Dr Nathan Shepherd coaxed her to hand the baby into his care. Holly was relieved to see Nathan. He was a skilled doctor, the fiancé of her friend Annie Webster—also a registrar in A&E—and she trusted him. So did Gus.

'We're expecting you. Come to Resus,' Nathan

instructed, cradling a red-faced Max, who was now struggling for each breath.

Hurrying behind him, with Gus at her side, Holly pressed her hands to her mouth, trying to stop the cries and pleas that wanted to burst from her. She was grateful when Gus gave Nathan a succinct if shaky account of events because she didn't think she could speak. The fear in Gus's voice matched her own. The speed of the swelling had shocked her, and she was wrestling with guilt. This was her fault. She'd left the door open. She'd brought the fruit in. And she'd known there were wasps around. She should have taken more care.

Seconds later they arrived in Resus, which was already busy with other patients. Holly knew they were only allowed to stay because of their connection to the department, so although the temptation to be close to Max was overwhelming she stood with Gus, out of the way. Feeling sick with anxiety, they watched and waited.

Nathan examined Max with brisk efficiency, the team following his directions for the administration of adrenalin via a nebuliser, followed by steroids and antihistamine to counteract the

swelling. Holly knew how good her former colleagues were, and she placed her trust in them to
save the baby she loved with all her heart.

As an oxygen mask was placed over Max's swol-
len face Gus slid an arm around her shoulders and
drew her close. Shaking from head to toe, and too
scared to think what she was doing, she turned
into him, seeking the comfort she so desperately
needed. Burying her face in his chest, she in-
haled his familiar scent, drawing on his strength.
Knowing he shared her fear, she wrapped her
arms around his waist and held on tight.

'I'm so sorry, Gus,' she sobbed. 'You must hate
me. It's all my fault.'

He stroked her hair with the palm of one hand,
gentle and soothing. 'That's nonsense, Holly.'

'I knew there were wasps around. I just didn't
think,' she continued, riddled with guilt.

'I saw them, too, and it didn't occur to me, either.'

'But—'

Much to her surprise, Gus drew back and
cupped her face in his hands, smoky green eyes
intense. 'Stop tormenting yourself. No one is
blaming you, darling, least of all me,' he re-

assured her. The endearment startled her and warmed her at the same time. 'It was a freak accident. That's *all*. I know you're frightened. I am, too. But Nathan knows what he's doing and Max will be all right.'

'He has to be,' she whispered, taken aback when Gus pressed a kiss to her forehead, leaving her skin tingling.

His hands dropped to her shoulders and turned her so she could see what was happening on the treatment table. Max had stopped crying, and she realised with a huge wave of relief that the swelling was lessening and his breathing improving. Nathan gestured to them and they followed him out of Resus into the relative quiet of the corridor. 'Max is doing well. He had five mg of nebulised adrenalin to begin with. We did anaesthetic and ENT reviews, but in the end he didn't need intubation or an emergency tracheotomy because he responded to the adrenalin, steroids and antihistamine we gave him,' he told them with a smile, and Holly sagged against Gus, clinging tenaciously to his hand, her fingers linked with his. 'He's settled, and the swelling is much reduced, so we're moving him to a quiet cubicle to rest, but it's close enough to bring him back to Resus in the unlikely event we need to. There's the potential of a second stage of reaction in the first six hours, but I'm not anticipating any problems.'

'Can we stay with him?' Holly asked, her voice rough with emotion.

Nathan nodded. 'Of course. And if his recovery continues like this you can take Max home—as soon as it's clear there'll be no further reaction. If he needs it overnight he can have some Calpol, but I think you'll find him back to normal by tomorrow.'

'Thank you.' Gus sounded as relieved as she felt, and she watched as he shook Nathan's hand. 'Do you think Max is now sensitised to wasp stings?'

'I believe this has been a localised reaction to being stung in a sensitive place inside the mouth and not a full-on anaphylactic attack,' Nathan explained, his brow creasing in concentration. 'As you know, generally a person needs to be stung once to sensitise the immune system, and it's after the second sting that an allergic response occurs. As far as we know Max has never been stung before.'

'And hopefully won't be again,' Holly interjected with feeling, and Gus's fingers gave hers a squeeze.

Nathan smiled in sympathy. 'It must have been a dreadful experience for both of you. We can do some tests at a later date to see if Max is sensitised or not, and you can carry an Epipen of adrenalin as a precaution, but my hunch is that this was a one-off event.'

'Thanks, Nathan…for everything,' she said with feeling.

Smiling, the handsome doctor gave her a quick hug. 'No worries.'

'How's Annie? I keep meaning to ring her or meet up for a chat.'

'She'd love that,' Nathan confirmed. 'She's much happier now the court case is over and her attacker is safely behind bars.'

'Thank God,' Gus responded, voicing aloud her own feelings.

Holly shivered, recalling the January day when Annie had been stabbed in A&E by a man escaping the police. Holly had transferred to the Children's Ward shortly before the event, but she'd visited Annie many times during her recovery and would never forget how close they'd come to losing her. It was a huge relief to know it was over and that the man would be serving a long sentence for nearly ending Annie's life.

Nathan gave further reassurances about Max's condition before saying goodbye to them both. Thankful that what had begun in such a scary and traumatic fashion was ending so happily, Holly accompanied Gus to the nearby cubicle where they found a much more contented Max. With tears welling in her eyes, Holly kissed his soft, warm cheek and cuddled him.

Gus's arms closed around them both in a three-way hug. Every atom of her being was aware of him and reacted to his closeness, reminding her how vulnerable she was to him and how easy it would be to let down her guard.

After the short but terrifying ordeal Max was safe.

Where Gus was concerned, Holly knew *she* was anything but.

Gus knew the instant he walked into the living room that Holly had been crying. And he could tell by the wobbly, over-bright smile and the characteristically stubborn lift of her chin that she was determined to hide it. He was equally determined to find out what had upset her. She didn't meet his gaze, focusing instead on the pillowcase she was ironing, folding it with studied care and adding it to the completed pile of laundry on the dining table behind her.

'Everything OK?' he asked, keeping his voice light as he dropped the things he was carrying on the sofa—including a plush teddy bear. He knelt on the floor to say hello to Max, who was lying on his play mat gym, happily kicking his legs and gurgling along to the music of a well-known nursery rhyme.

'Fine.' Holly's answer was predictable, and he didn't believe her, but he allowed her to temporarily divert his attention back to his son. 'Given all the kicking practice he's been doing, I think Max is going to be a footballer when he grows up.'

He smiled, drawing the growing baby into his arms. 'Yeah?'

'He's learned two new things today,' she continued, pride mixing with the false jollity in her voice.

'That's great.'

Max had made a full and swift recovery from the wasp sting, and after their return from the hospital had slept through the night, appearing none the worse for his adventures come morning. Gus smiled ruefully…he and Holly had been the unsettled ones. He felt as if he'd aged ten years.

Gus gave Max a kiss and set him back on the mat to play. 'Are you going to show Papa your new moves?'

'He's been doing mini-press-ups. And he's discovered how to work the buzzer,' Holly told him, her smile more natural as Max chose that moment to demonstrate his new skill and happily smacked the button to ring the buzzer.

Laughing, Gus rose to his feet. 'Nice one, half-pint!'

He loved these moments, coming home from work full of eager anticipation at seeing Max. And Holly. Since Max had been stung he and Holly had shared a new closeness, brought together by their shared fear, giving each other strength and comfort. The underlying tension and awareness simmering beneath the surface was also increasing all the time. It was becoming harder and harder to hide his feelings from Holly…and to remember that unresolved issues lay between them. At times he was convinced Holly felt the attraction, too, but she'd rejected him once before and he was wary of making another mistake and being hurt again.

'Who's your friend?' Holly asked, breaking into his reverie. 'He's gorgeous.'

'It's not meant for children under three, but I couldn't resist when I discovered the bear was called Max,' he confided, closing the distance between them and handing her the super-soft, hand-made teddy.

'I can cuddle him until Max takes over.'

If ever anyone looked in need of a cuddle it was Holly. As she hugged the bear tightly Gus struggled to resist the temptation to step around the ironing board and wrap her in his arms. First he needed to uncover the cause of her discomfort. But he knew from past experience that coming right out and asking wouldn't work.

'I'm going upstairs to change,' he told her, noting her cheeks were so pale that her cute smattering of freckles stood out in stark relief. 'Shall I take the laundry up with me?'

'That would be great, thanks.'

Her hands shook as she sat the teddy bear on the table before picking up the neatly ironed pile of bedlinens and towels. Their fingers brushed as she transferred the bundle to him, and he was surprised to see a bloom of colour return to her cheeks. Surprised and intrigued. Flustered, she stepped back, lowering the ironing board and hiding behind it as if it were a shield.

He was almost at the door when a thought nagged him and he half turned to address her. 'I didn't get a chance to tell you this morning, but I found a photo album before I went to work. Did you see it?'

'Yes.' Sooty lashes hid her expression. 'Thank you.'

The falsely cheery tone of her voice didn't fool him for a minute. 'Holly, what's wrong?'

'Nothing.' Her smile frayed at the edges. 'I'm just tired.'

It was a lie and they both knew it. As she disappeared into the kitchen Gus went upstairs, considering how to get her to talk to him. He put the laundry in the airing cupboard, then continued down the corridor. As he passed Holly's room he automatically glanced inside the open door, his footsteps slowing as he noticed the photo album lying on the floor.

Rather than falling accidentally, it had clearly been roughly pushed aside. Holly had been anxious to get the pictures back, so why had she discarded it? Was this what had upset her? Had he given her the wrong thing? In his haste that morning he hadn't looked at the contents.

Concern for her overriding his caution, he crossed the threshold of her room and picked up the book. As he began to scan the pages the cause of Holly's distress was obvious. Gus swore under his breath, his throat tightening as anger welled within him. In each photograph Holly's face, and that of her mother, had either been cut out or mutilated and defaced with nasty words or scribbling. There was no doubt that Julia had been the guilty party, but why had she been so vindictive? He had no answers, only more questions.

Uppermost in his mind was Holly, and how she must have felt when she'd seen the pictures. She'd longed for them—only to discover them in this state. He felt horribly guilty for not checking to ensure there was nothing to upset her. Not that he could ever have foreseen *this*.

Holly was back in the dining room, sorting a pile of Max's Babygros and she looked surprised when she saw him. 'I thought you were going to get changed.'

'I was. But…'

He put the album on the table, hearing her soft exclamation of distress. Breaking his rule not to touch her, he cupped her face in his hands and tilted her head up so he could see the pain and shimmer of tears in her beautiful blue eyes.

'I'm so sorry, Holly. I would *never* have let you see this if I'd known.'

Tears pooled before spilling past her lashes and trailing down her cheeks. 'Gus…'

As a ragged sob shuddered through her, tearing at his heart, he drew her into his arms. She felt so right. A perfect fit. And as he breathed in he noticed how good she smelled. Uniquely Holly… feminine, subtle but sultry and sexy, like a wild-flower meadow on a warm summer day. As her arms stole around his waist and she leaned into him, crying out the hurt, he held her tight, uncaring that her tears soaked through his shirt to his skin.

'I understand how awful it must have been for Julia to lose her mother at such a young age, and then to see her father remarry and have me—but even after everything else she's done I wasn't prepared for the photos,' she sobbed brokenly, and a knot formed in his chest in response to her pain. 'Mum and Dad tried so hard with her, but instead of mellowing as she grew older her resentment increased.'

Gus slid a hand under the silken strands of her hair, his fingers stroking the whisper-soft skin of her neck. A shaky sigh escaped her and she leaned against him, some of the tension draining from her as her tears slowed.

'What else did she do?' he asked, keeping his voice low as he encouraged her to talk, unable to doubt her sincerity or the reality of Julia's actions.

She was silent for several moments and he held his breath, giving her time, hoping she would confide in him and explain some of the many things he didn't understand. Haltingly, Holly outlined examples of the unkind acts and petty jealousies Julia had been responsible for when they

were growing up, and he was amazed and impressed that Holly remained so compassionate
and forgiving.

But learning about Julia's more recent actions
shocked him even more.

'Julia was seventeen when our father died,
and she went into a rage when she discovered
she was unable to challenge his will,' Holly explained. 'Dad loved her so much, but he wasn't
blind to her faults, and he made sure my mother
was provided for and our house was protected
while Mum was alive.'

'I should hope so,' he murmured, his fingers
continuing their caress of her skin. How could
Julia have been so unreasonable?

'Julia didn't agree. She left Strathlochan—
went working as a beauty therapist on cruise
ships. She boasted about the lifestyle, the status,
the money. When Mum became ill with Motor
Neurone Disease Julia wasn't interested. I'd orig-
inally wanted to be a doctor,' she confided, surprising him anew, 'but looking after Mum was
my priority, so I stayed home and trained to be
a nurse instead, because I could do that here in
Strathlochan.'

His heart ached for her. 'I'm sorry, darling, that's such a cruel disease,' he sympathised, the endearment slipping out as he imagined all she and her mother must have been through together.

'Yes.' She paused a moment, sucking in a steadying breath before continuing. 'After Mum died Julia returned to claim her share of the estate. I really didn't want to lose the only home I'd ever known, so I took out a mortgage, which enabled me to pay Julia her half, but she was never satisfied with that. She saw herself as Dad's *proper* daughter and entitled to everything.'

'That's ridiculous.'

'It's how she felt.' She glanced up at him with a sad smile, and the expression in her blue eyes made him feel as if he'd been punched in the gut. 'Other things happened then...'

Gus felt a flicker of unease as he recalled one of the things Julia had told him about Holly's past. He wanted to know the truth, yet part of him feared what he might learn. 'You and Euan were going to be married?' he finally asked, noting the flash of disquiet in her eyes before sooty lashes lowered to mask them.

'What did Julia tell you?' she countered, a wary reserve evident.

'Not much.' He remembered all too well the fateful night when Holly had stood him up and Julia, amongst other things, had told him that Holly had a track record in breaking hearts. 'No real details—just that you'd called things off at the last minute.'

Gus frowned as he thought back to the conversation with Julia. At the time he'd been so wounded and disillusioned at the way Holly had rejected *him* that Julia's revelations about Euan had hurt, sketchy though they had been, although the image of Holly being cold and thoughtless didn't fit with the woman he knew.

'We *were* supposed to be married,' she confirmed, a new tension in her voice.

He experienced an irrational curl of jealousy. 'What happened?'

'I called off the wedding a month before it was due to take place.' She paused, and he felt the quiver that rippled through her. 'After I came home and found Euan in bed with someone else. But I don't want to talk about it,' she added with a quiet dignity that tightened his chest. 'Raking over the details serves no purpose.'

He believed her, understanding why she'd acted as she had. And why she shied away from talking about it now, much as he would have liked to know more. The man had been crazy to risk losing Holly by doing something so unforgivable, and it was obvious the betrayal had hurt her and broken her trust. 'I'm sorry. He was an idiot to throw away what he had with you.'

As his fingers stroked her skin and she leaned into him he reflected on how Holly's version cast a very different light on the story than the one Julia had wanted him to believe. He was frustrated; he still didn't understand *why*.

'I didn't see Julia again until she came home—supposedly sorry for the way she had treated Mum and me. She claimed to be in terrible trouble,' Holly continued with a shake of her head. She sighed deeply. 'It was a shock to learn she'd become addicted to gambling on the cruise ships she'd worked on, and was heavily in debt to the wrong kind of people. She said she'd been threatened and she feared what would happen if she didn't find the money. She begged me to help her.'

Gus swore softly under his breath. 'And you did.' He knew at once that Holly would have gone above and beyond, no matter what had happened in the past.

'I was stupid to believe her.'

'You weren't stupid,' he chided gently. 'You care about family. And Julia took advantage of your kind and forgiving nature.'

Holly sighed, resting her head on his chest. 'She had me hook, line and sinker. James Russell, the solicitor, cautioned me against the loan but I was ridiculously naïve…and I wanted to believe her.' She gave a humourless laugh. 'I was *so* wrong. The house was sold and I "loaned" Julia the money. Once it was too late she came clean and told me I'd never see a penny of it again.'

'You should have sued her.' Even as he said the words he knew she never would have done it and he suspected Julia had known it, too. Anger burned inside him at the injustice and hurt Holly had endured.

'Probably—but I couldn't have faced airing the family's dirty deeds in public. For the sake of my parents' memories as much as for my embarrass-ment,' she explained, confirming his thoughts. 'Julia saw the money as rightfully hers. As there's nothing left for Max, I guess she used it to fund the lavish lifestyle she'd become accustomed to.'

Which was what James Russell had been refer-ring to when they'd met him to discuss Julia's af-fairs, Gus realised. 'So you moved into George's house?'

'Yes. I had nothing left,' she said, with stark simplicity but none of the bitterness most people would have justly displayed. 'George and I had been friends since childhood and she stepped in to help me.'

Gus felt ashamed to have been so taken in by Julia, ignoring his own instincts about Holly. He looked at his son, dozing contentedly on his play mat. He could never regret Max, but he regretted many other things.

'For a while I clung to the dream of buying the house back, but I've resigned myself to the fact that it will never happen,' she confided wistfully.

In that moment, although he had no idea how or when, he vowed to do all he could to make Holly's dream come true. And to make real a bigger dream of his own—that one day he, Holly and Max would live in that house together, be their own family. If that were ever to be more than a fantasy he needed to win Holly round, to find out what had gone wrong and why she had rejected him. He was no longer sure he could believe anything Julia had told him.

As Holly drew back, Gus reluctantly loosened his hold. She looked up at him, an endearingly puzzled expression on her face, and he tucked a stray wisp of wavy blonde hair back behind her ear. Disobedient fingers lingered, relishing the feel of her baby-soft skin as they trailed their way along her jawline. Sky-blue eyes darkened and he felt a tremor run through her as he traced the plumpness of her lower lip with the pad of his thumb.

He heard the hitch in her breath. The rapid beat of her pulse matched his own, and as she swayed towards him temptation won and he forgot all the reasons why this was a bad idea. He couldn't wait another second to kiss her. Anticipation and excitement coursed through his veins as the distance between them closed. Finally, after waiting what felt like for ever, his lips met hers.

Savouring the moment, he began a leisurely journey of discovery, learning the shape of her, the feel of her, the taste of her. She whimpered as he teased the seam of her lips with his tongue.

Just when he was on the point of finding out what it was like to kiss her properly, Max ruined the moment.

The shrill sound of the buzzer from the play mat nearby was a sudden intrusion—one that had both of them tensing. Skittish, Holly drew away from him. The disappointment was huge. She'd been with him, he knew it, and as eager as he, but now the moment of intimacy was lost.

As she stepped away and gathered Max into her arms Gus wondered when he might have another opportunity to hold her, to kiss her—to admit to her, as he had to himself, that his feelings had never changed. Indeed, they had grown even stronger. He knew without doubt that he loved her. But he had no idea how she felt about him.

CHAPTER ELEVEN

HAVING stopped by the nursery to check on Max, who was sleeping soundly, Holly hovered outside the bathroom door. She had never in her life gone to bed at night without removing her make-up or brushing her teeth, and she didn't want to start now. But she was dog-tired after covering extra hours at the hospital…and Gus was in the bathroom. In the *bath*.

Since their kiss had been interrupted by Max two evenings ago the tension between Gus and herself had been electric. Regret and relief vied within her. Regret was winning. But no matter how much she loved Gus, she would always be second best. That he'd chosen Julia—and now grieved for her—was a barrier she couldn't overcome.

She walked a few steps towards her bedroom, then hesitated and tiptoed back to the bathroom, caught in an agony of indecision.

'Is there a problem?'

Oh, hell! Holly froze at the sound of Gus's voice.

'Holly?'

'It's OK. Sorry. I didn't mean to bother you.'

'You're not bothering me.' There was a moment's pause. 'Did you want to come in?'

'No!' Holly closed her eyes, pressing her palms to her cheeks, as if in doing so she could stop them blushing. 'I was just going to bed and...'

'If you want to brush your teeth or something you can come in and do it,' he invited, as if it was the most normal thing in the world.

She couldn't go in there! On the other hand, they were both adults, and if Gus didn't mind why should she?

'Holly?'

'Um...are you sure that's OK?' she asked, half hoping he'd say no.

'It's fine. I'm decent.'

That was a matter of opinion! 'All right.'

Her heart in her mouth, her fingers closed around the door handle. She slowly opened it and stepped inside, determined to keep her gaze averted and *not* look at Gus. The water sloshed softly as he moved. Oh, God! Standing at the basin, she could see the bath out of the corner of her eye. Her fingers tightened their grip on the vanity unit as she tried to ignore the images her wayward imagination was conjuring up. Of Gus. In the bath. *Naked*.

It was very hot in here!

Aware of him watching her, she set about washing her face. Her fingers shook as she applied cleanser and then used a soft muslin cloth to remove her light make-up and all traces of the day. She went through each step of her routine in record time and brushed her teeth before finally applying her night cream. The sooner she finished the better—before she succumbed to the temptation to look at Gus. Or, worse, threw caution to the wind and climbed into the bath with him!

Gus watched in fascination as Holly went through her night-time routine. She looked incredibly young. Fresh-faced and natural and lovely. Her sleeveless T-shirt fell short of her knees and rode up further as she stretched to reach the bathroom cabinet, giving him a brief view of curvy, creamy thighs. He shifted lower in the water, thankful that Holly had no idea of his body's instinctive reaction to her.

He was both relieved and disappointed when her tasks were completed and she moved towards the door. She hesitated, and for the first time her gaze strayed in his direction, a rosy glow pinkening her freshly washed cheeks.

'Thanks, Gus.'

'No problem.'

He sighed as she slipped out of the room and closed the door, apparently far less affected by the situation than he had been. Disgruntled and unsettled, he removed the plug, climbed out of the bath and towelled himself dry. After knotting the towel around his waist, he went to brush his teeth and found Holly's wristwatch beside the basin. His fingers hovered over it. He could just leave it for her to find. He could just tell her it was there. Or he could give it back to her himself and know it was safe.

The excuse to see her was impossible to resist and he picked up the watch.

Holly closed her bedroom door and leaned back against it, pressing her palms to her flushed,

overheated cheeks. She'd escaped, but not before she'd broken her resolve and stolen a last-
minute look at Gus. The sight of him reclining
in the sudsy water was imprinted on her brain,
making her all hot and bothered. She closed her
eyes, but the image of broad shoulders, muscled
arms and tanned, glistening wet skin remained.
He was gorgeous. Just thinking about him made
a hunger burn within her, and the aching, needy
knot that was all too familiar a response to him
squeezed ever more tightly.

A knock sounded on the door she was leaning on, and with a squeal of surprise she jumped
away from it.

'Holly?' Puzzlement and concern laced Gus's
husky voice. 'Are you OK?'

'Fine. J-Just a minute,' she called, battling for
composure.

Turning round, she smoothed the hem of her
sleep-shirt down her thighs. It was too late to
worry about it; he'd already seen her wearing it.
With a rueful shake of her head, she acknowledged that Gus wouldn't notice if she was in her
birthday suit. She opened the door, her breath
catching as her greedy gaze drank in the sight

of him wearing nothing but a towel slung low over his hips.

'You forgot this,' he told her.

He held out a hand, her wristwatch nestling in its palm. She'd been so keen to escape the bath-room—and Gus—she'd left it behind.

'Thanks,' she murmured, her voice unsteady.

She edged closer, all too aware of the clean male scent of him and the familiar fragrance of his soap. Her fingers closed around the watch. His fingers closed around hers, his touch sending a dart of fire up her arm. She was in trouble. She swallowed, her attention caught as a single drop-let of water trickled down his skin. Captivated, she couldn't drag her gaze away as it followed the path of the narrow line of dark hair down his abdomen to his navel. She licked her lips, fight-ing the overwhelming craving to lean in and lick it from his skin.

'Holly...'

The sexy roughness of his voice tightened her insides. She dragged her reluctant gaze back up his lean, muscled torso to the feathering of dark hair between the bronze orbs of his nipples. Her heart was hammering by the time her gaze roamed up the column of his throat and handsome face to meet his. The sultry expression in smoky green eyes stole any remaining breath from her lungs.

Tension and awareness sizzled in the air. His gaze roved slowly from her face to her toes and back again. Every particle of her felt energised, as if he were touching her. Her nipples peaked against the thin cotton that covered them and he couldn't help but notice her arousal.

He looked into her eyes and she feared what he would see. Need. Want. Desire. She was too tired to hide her feelings. Too tired to fight. But seeing her emotions mirrored in his eyes amazed and excited her, and severed the last of her resistance to temptation.

Holly swayed towards him as if pulled by an invisible magnet. His free hand rose, his fingers brushing her skin before spearing into her hair and fisting in the unruly waves. A needy whimper escaped as his mouth claimed hers, taking possession as a blaze of fiery passion exploded between them, shocking her and driving Julia and every other reason why she shouldn't be doing this from her mind.

There was no uncertainty, no hesitation, only a sense of rightness, of homecoming, of belonging. Her previous experience was limited to Euan, but what she'd once felt for him was tame compared to the raging love, need and want she knew with Gus. His taste was intoxicating. Her tongue explored, gliding and twining with his as the kiss deepened. The desperation to be closer was overwhelming. She pressed herself against him, excited by the feel of his warm damp skin. But it wasn't enough. She wanted, *needed*, more. And he knew. As he curled an arm around her hips and lifted her, her legs encircled him and she wriggled against him, feeling the evidence of his arousal.

She protested as he broke the kiss. Both of them were breathing heavily. She tried to reclaim his mouth but he evaded her and her eyes opened in confusion, her heart turning over as she encountered the raw passion blazing in his.

'Gus?'

'I need you, Holly.'

A sensual shiver ran through her. She loved him. She'd wanted him for so long. And she could deny him nothing. 'Yes.'

As she surrendered to the inevitable, his hold on her tightened. She clung to him as he carried her down the corridor, past the nursery where Max slept soundly and into his own room, where the baby listening device would warn them if they were needed. She felt a momentary flicker of unease as thoughts of Julia intruded, but Gus held all her attention as he set her on her feet and drew the sleep-shirt slowly up her body and over her head. The hunger of his gaze and the reverence of his touch as he shaped the contours of her body with his hands brought a bloom of heat all over.

'You're so beautiful, Holly.'

Feeling it for the first time in her life, and emboldened by his desire for her, she trailed her fingers down his chest and abdomen to the towel encasing his hips. She loosened it, allowing it to fall to the floor. With a quiver of desire she drank in the sight of him in full masculine glory.

'So are you,' she told him with equal sincerity and excited anticipation as her fingers shyly but lovingly shaped him, learning the feel of him.

As Gus laid her on his bed and followed her down Holly could think of nothing but him and this moment. She had no idea what would happen tomorrow, and although she feared this would fundamentally change things for ever for once she didn't care. She couldn't think that far ahead. She would deal with the consequences when they came.

For this night the man she loved was hers. She vowed to cast her worries aside, to live every moment, store every memory…and show Gus in every way she could without words what he meant to her.

Meeting and matching the fervour of his kiss, she gave herself up to the magic of the passion that consumed them. His touch turned her molten, the seductiveness of his mouth drove her wild, and every molecule, cell and neuron in her body responded to him. Inhibitions evaporated and she yielded to the driving need that overwhelmed them and flared out of control. As the force of the sensual, erotic storm reached a crescendo it sent them soaring over the edge together, free-falling into oblivion.

Dragging a hand through his hair, Gus watched from an upstairs window as Holly, pushing Max in his buggy, walked down the leafy road away from the house and disappeared from view.

He was confused. Riddled with doubt. And the cold fist of fear that had formed when he'd woken and found himself alone in bed tightened more forcefully inside him. Following the most amazing night of his life, after which he'd assumed things with Holly would be back on track and a permanent relationship would grow, she was—again—in retreat.

Skittish and jumpy, she hadn't been able to wait to put distance between them. What had gone wrong? Had he misjudged things? Was Holly as fearful of commitment as Julia had claimed and about to reject him a second time?

Last night had been a new experience for him. In the past he'd always been controlled and uninvolved, holding an elemental part of himself back, but with Holly things were different. With her there had been no emotional or physical barriers. He'd laid every part of himself bare to her, surrendered his soul, exposed his heart. He'd thought Holly had done the same. She'd shown an endearing mix of innocence and adventurousness, responding with passionate abandon.

He wanted her for ever, not just for one night. Because he loved her.

He loved her compassion, her intelligence, her kindness, her humour. He admired her loyalty, her devotion to Max, her dedication to her patients, her determination to see any challenge through without allowing anything to beat her. Despite all the pain caused to her Holly had remained fair, generous and forgiving where Julia was concerned. He loved that she shared his taste in music, books and films, that they shared the same outlook on life, and that they could talk about anything for hours, or could be just as comfortable with silence. He loved her responsiveness, the way their bodies were so attuned, so compatible. They shared a respect, an implicit and instinctive trust.

In the rosy glow after making love to her for the second time he'd told her he wanted them to be together, a real family. She hadn't responded and he'd thought she'd fallen asleep. Now he knew she'd been evading him, and he had no more idea of how she felt about him now than he had before their passionate night together.

Having woken alone, he'd showered, dressed,

and gone in search of her, finding her in the kitchen with Max. As he'd crossed to her and wrapped his arms around her she'd wriggled free, sidestepping his kiss. Doubt and fear had replaced the hope and joy of last night.

'What's wrong?' he'd asked, picking Max up and cuddling him.

'Nothing.'

The lie had tightened the knot in his chest. 'I thought last night meant something to you.'

'It did. Does,' she'd amended hastily. 'But…'

'But what?' he'd pressed, hardly daring to breathe.

'I need to think.' Her voice was shaky, her eyes bright with unshed tears. 'Please, Gus.'

He'd struggled to make sense of things. 'Think about what? I don't understand. I hoped this was the start of more for us. We'd make a good family.'

'I don't know if I can get past you and Julia—knowing you were with her and that I'm second best.'

'You're not!' Her words had shocked him to the core. She couldn't believe that, surely? 'Why would you think that?'

She'd bitten her lip. 'You chose her, not me. You had a baby with her. You're grieving for her,' she'd pointed out, her words whisper-soft and yet hitting him like hammer-blows.

'Holly—'

His protest had died in his throat as he'd struggled to take in not just the words she'd spoken but the messages that lay behind them. It wasn't the first time she'd implied that he'd chosen Julia over her. It wasn't true. Holly had stood him up and made it clear she didn't want him—yet the way she spoke anyone would think it was the other way around! Given the support he'd received since the accident, how could he admit that he'd never loved Julia and wasn't consumed by grief? He'd sound like the most thoughtless, unfeeling bastard ever.

He'd been wrestling with his thoughts when Holly had spoken again, her cheeks flushed, sooty lashes lowered to hide her emotions.

'I care about you,' she'd confided softly. 'I love Max with all my heart. But every time I look at him I think of you and Julia together, and...' She'd paused, one hand pressed to her stomach, her sky-blue eyes full of pain. 'There are things you don't know,' she'd added cryptically. 'I can't help how I feel, Gus. I need time to know if I can deal with this. For all our sakes.'

He'd had little option but to agree and give Holly the time she'd asked for. But he didn't like it.

Now, as she took Max out to meet Callie and Izzy at Annie's house, Gus went to the master bedroom to continue sorting Julia's belongings. Everything was so complicated. All he could do was wait…wait and pray that Holly truly cared for him, and that her love for Max was enough for her to see beyond the past to the future that could lie ahead of them.

They needed to talk. He had to lay the truth on the table once and for all. Not just that he loved her and always had, but what had happened with Julia…the state of his marriage, even his version of events on the night Max had been conceived. And he wanted to know from Holly why she'd stood him up, why she'd sent Julia to meet him, and why she'd never explained or apologised afterwards. And then there were the 'things' she'd alluded to…the *things he didn't know*. What were they? Were they an insurmountable obstacle to them being together?

Engrossed in his thoughts, he pulled too hard on the drawer in Julia's bedside cabinet and only just caught it before it hit the floor. As he lifted it to slide it back onto its runners he discovered a large envelope taped to the underside of the drawer. Frowning, he felt inside and pulled out a leather-bound journal.

He flicked the journal open and recognised Julia's handwriting. Any initial awkwardness he felt at the invasion of her privacy evaporated as some of the entries jumped out at him…nasty remarks and jealous resentment directed at Holly. He discovered that it had been *Julia* who had been in bed with Euan, Holly's fiancé, leading to the cancellation of the wedding. Holly had shielded him from *that* information, he realised, believing he had loved Julia. He burned with anger at what Julia had done to betray her sister, but at the same time he felt deeply ashamed that he'd ever been taken in by her.

What else had Julia lied about? He flicked through the journal to the night he and Julia had met. The night he should have been on his first

proper date with Holly. The night Julia had told
him Holly didn't want him.

There, in black and white, Julia's words revealed the shocking truth...

*Things turned out so much better than I ex-
pected. I only meant to spoil Holly's date with
Gus, but when he went to get me a drink and
I discovered he'd left his mobile phone behind it was the simplest thing to send Holly a
text cancelling the evening. I'd love to have
seen her face when it arrived just as she
must have been leaving home! Thank God I
had time to delete the message and Holly's
pathetic reply from his phone before he came
back... So Gus was none the wiser. Likewise
Holly. And with Gus unwell it was easy to
convince him of Holly's duplicity. As far as
he was concerned she'd stood him up with
no explanation!*

*It was obvious from talking to Gus how much
they care about each other and I knew one
missed date wasn't going to upset things
for long. A few questions the next day and
it would be obvious what happened. That's*

when the idea came to me. I'd had no intention of doing anything more, but with Gus so ill things played into my hands and I just ran with it, acting on instinct. It's amazing what desperation can drive you to do. Suddenly I saw a way out of the mess I'm in. And if it works it'll kill two birds with one stone... solving my own dilemma whilst at the same time messing things up for Miss Goody-Two-Shoes. Always a bonus.

Julia's maliciousness appalled him. He'd blamed Holly for things going wrong and for rejecting him, but all the time *she* must have been blaming *him*. Holly had never sent Julia to the Strathlochan Arms in her place. Holly had received a cancellation text she'd believed was from him, and then she'd learned from gossip that he'd spent the evening with her sister. No wonder she'd been hurt and angry. And had assumed he'd chosen Julia over her.

Damn Julia and her lies. Why had she done it? Shaking his head, he looked back over the journal entry and frowned. What had Julia meant about solving her own dilemma? Irate and puzzled, he sat on the bed and turned the pages, needing to learn more. But as he read one horrifying entry after another, the blood chilled in his veins and his whole world crashed down around him.

Having forced herself to act normally with Annie, Callie and baby Izzy—who, with her shock of red hair and her mother's startling violet eyes, was developing a firecracker personality—Holly headed home with a characteristically laid-back Max. She felt far from relaxed, however, as her nervousness about facing Gus increased.

After the most incredible night of her life, during which Gus had told her he wanted them to be a family, she'd woken in the morning confused and unsettled. Everything she most wanted was hers for the taking, so she should have jumped at the chance. But she couldn't. Because, as she'd told Gus, no matter how she felt about him she couldn't get out of her head the fact that he'd been with Julia. And if she entered into a relationship with Gus, uncertain whether she could live with it, what chance would they have?

He'd said she wasn't second best, but however much she wanted to believe that the evidence pointed to the contrary. Gus had chosen to be with Julia, to have a baby with her. And it still hurt. So much. She felt guilty for feeling so jealous and upset—especially given the tragedy that had befallen her sister. As for Gus, she knew he would do what he thought was best for Max. So did Gus really want *her*? Or did he just want to secure a mother for his son? She feared the latter while dreaming the former was true. But how would she *know*?

If it had been anyone but Julia maybe she could have put it behind her. But her sister…? A shiver ran through her. What else had Julia told Gus about her? She thought of his questions about her cancelled wedding. Julia had taken a fragment of the truth, twisted it to give a very different impression, and left Gus to believe the blame lay with Holly, not Euan.

Euan. Her childhood sweetheart. The man she'd planned to marry. And, until last night, the only man she'd ever slept with. She hadn't told Gus the full truth about the betrayal that had led her to call off the wedding. Why hurt Gus, who was grieving for his lost wife, by telling him what Julia had done? Nothing could change the past.

Just as she could never fully recover from what had happened a week or two after finding Euan and Julia together. The skeleton in her cupboard that no one but Julia and her GP knew about. Pain ripped through her as the memories returned. Even after all this time tears threatened, and the dreadful hollow void deep inside remained. Could she tell Gus the full story? She didn't know. But she could never start a relationship with undisclosed secrets hanging in the air—just as she could never forget that Gus had chosen Julia and that Max, however beloved, was his and Julia's son.

She was going round in circles. Sighing, she walked up the path. Opening the front door, she reversed in, better able to guide Max's buggy through the porch and into the hall. Closing the door, she turned round, halting in surprise.

Ashen-faced, Gus was sitting near the foot of the staircase watching her.

Unease was replaced by the cold weight of dread as she met his gaze and saw the despair and pain that dulled his smoky green eyes.

CHAPTER TWELVE

'Gus? What is it?' As he stared at her in silence Holly pressed a hand to her chest, where a knot of anxiety had formed. 'You're scaring me. What's wrong?'

Slowly he rose to his feet, and for the first time she noticed the leather-bound book in his hands. He walked down the final steps and handed it over, before slipping past her and opening the front door.

'Read it,' he instructed, his voice disturbingly flat and devoid of emotion.

As the door closed behind him Holly hesitated, unsure whether to do as he had asked or go after him to ensure he was all right. Concerned for him, and needing to understand what had upset him, she went into the living room, her thoughts confused.

After taking Max out of his buggy, Holly gave him a kiss and a cuddle, then settled him on his play-mat. Dropping her bag on the floor beside her, she sat in an armchair and opened the book at the page Gus had marked. Immediately she recognised Julia's handwriting. Puzzlement turned to shocked disbelief as she read her sister's journal.

Holly gasped as she discovered it had been *Julia* who had sent the message from Gus's mobile phone to cancel the date that fateful autumn night. Gus had known nothing about the text, nor her reply to it, Julia having deleted the evidence. Anger, pain and regret filled her. Whilst she'd blamed him for what had happened, Gus had believed *she* had coldly and calculatingly stood *him* up. No wonder he'd been so strange with her.

Both she and Gus had been hurt, each seeking explanations the other had been unable to give, each feeling the other had staged a humiliating public rejection…just as Julia had wanted. And with so many of their colleagues in the Strathlochan Arms as witnesses the subsequent hospital gossip had driven the wedge more deeply between Gus and herself, completing the job her sister had started.

The ache inside her turned to sick despair as she read more of the journal entries…

I hadn't thought further ahead than sabotaging Holly's date, but then Paul and I rowed so terribly that afternoon… I was panicked. I didn't know what to do. Unlike Holly, I've never wanted to be a mother. When I first realised I was pregnant I had every intention of having an abortion as Paul demanded. I was shocked when I went into the clinic and found I couldn't go through with it. I didn't want the baby and I didn't want to lose Paul, but I just couldn't do it. I just couldn't kill it. Paul was so furious. He kept accusing me of trying to trap him… It's not true. It was an accident…a condom failure—ironic, given what I said to Holly after her miscarriage.

Holly pressed her fingers to her mouth, fighting back a sob as she relived the terrifying and heartbreaking moment a couple of weeks after Euan's betrayal, when she had miscarried the baby she hadn't known she was carrying. The anguish and hollow ache of loss had never diminished, and the news of Julia's pregnancy had only increased her feelings of betrayal and jealousy.

'Don't you know anything about contraception?' Julia had sneered. 'Or the morning-after pill?'

'A condom must have split,' she'd explained, hating the way her beautiful, sophisticated older sister always belittled her, making her feel small and stupid.

'At least you've lost it and haven't had to arrange an abortion.'

Holly had been horrified 'I'd *never* have had an abortion,' she'd retaliated, distraught that this unexpected and all too brief new life had been extinguished.

'There's no way I'd be caught like that—or have a baby ruin my body.' Julia's tone had been characteristically patronising, her words wounding. 'It's different for you, Holly, you've always been plain and careless about your appearance.'

Shaking her head as she relived that painful conversation, Holly tried to push the memories from her mind and refocus on the journal…

Hopefully I can win Paul back when this is over. In the meantime, I'm facing the fright-

*ening prospect of doing it alone. Or was...
until I met Gus. I may not have planned it,
but when the opportunity arose, I went for
it. I know it's impulsive and mad, but it's
the best outcome for the baby. It was a risk,
but the stakes are high for me. I knew Gus
was living at the Strathlochan Arms so his
room was nearby. He was disorientated from
whatever virus he had. Apparently he doesn't
drink, and was taking medication, so I took
the chance and put loads of vodka in what
he assumed was water. He reacted so quickly
I was worried I'd overdone it, but I helped
him to his room, then got him undressed and
into bed before he passed out. Enough people saw us to spark some gossip that will hurt
Holly. Come morning, Gus had no memories of what had happened. I almost laughed
aloud at the horrified look on his face when
he woke to find me in bed with him!
So I feel I've done pretty well for myself! Not
only did I achieve my original aim of spoiling
things for Holly, but I've gained an insurance
policy and solved my problem. Given Gus's
sense of honour and responsibility, I knew*

he'd step up if he thought the baby was his.
What I never anticipated was his demand to
get married! In name only, thank God... But
even that has its benefits. He's taking care of
me in every way, and Holly's heartbroken,
thinking the relationship is real. Perfect.

'Oh, my God.'

Tears stung Holly's eyes as the evidence of her
sister's cruelty hit home. Never mind that Julia
had taken pleasure in ruining her chance at happiness—far worse was what she had done to Gus.
Months of lies, allowing Gus to believe he was
the baby's father. It explained so much—like how
wrong the due date had seemed. It *was* wrong—
but Gus hadn't known that.

It was so much fun at first—playing Holly
and Gus off against each other, letting Holly
believe Gus loved me and found her unat-
tractive. It's so easy to get to her—always
has been. I'm the beautiful one, but plain
podgy Holly always gets the attention be-
cause she's so good, *so* nice. *But I proved it*
was me *they all wanted—first Euan and now*

Gus. She has no idea that Gus and I have never slept together, that we live separate lives. And I'm not telling her. Not yet. Until the baby is born Holly can go on thinking that the man she loves really loves me.

Entry after entry was the same. Holly forced herself to read on, too stunned to take everything in. That Julia had planned to walk away once the baby was born was another shock revealed in later entries. She talked about the real father, Paul Dalziel...the man who'd been killed with his wife and whose funeral Julia had attended before her accident. It was clear Julia had loved the man who, it transpired, had been unable to leave the disabled wife who needed him. He had grown children and no wish for more, hence his rejection of the baby he'd made with Julia.

Despite past experience of her sister's schemes, Holly believed that the baby had indeed been an accident, and not a way to trap Paul into further commitment. Julia's intent was clear...the baby would stay with Gus while she returned to Paul. But that was not to be. Two tragic accidents had taken the lives of both Max's genetic parents.

There were signs in the final entries that Julia had been reflecting on the past, Holly discovered, wiping the tears that blurred her eyes…

I've done some terrible things. I see that now. And I regret them. I've always hated that Holly is so popular. Everyone loves her—especially Dad. He was mine before she came along. Holly's never had to try, whereas I've always found it hard to make friends. I do bad things to be noticed, to get attention, but the fact that my father, stepmother and Holly always forgive me somehow makes it worse. They make allowances for my behaviour, but what hurts me is the disappointment in their eyes when they look at me.

I can't repair the damage I've done. I feel bad because Gus is a nice man. Genuine. He's been good to me…and I've been a real bitch to him. I know he'll give the baby a happy life. I'll write to him—and Holly—telling them enough of the truth to maybe help repair their relationship. Whatever else I think of her, Holly was always perfect mother material. Unlike me. Now, though, I can under-

stand how she felt when she miscarried her own baby. Soon this nightmare will be over and I'll have my life...and Paul...back again.

Fate had intervened and prevented Julia from bringing her plans to fruition. Julia had struggled to come to terms with the news that Paul and his wife and been killed. On the outside she'd seemed like herself, but inside she'd gone to pieces. After attending the funeral, distraught and drinking to mask the pain, she'd crashed the car with inevitable consequences.

Her cheeks wet with tears, Holly dropped to her knees and cuddled Max, needing him close. She breathed in his familiar scent, giving thanks for the umpteenth time that he'd survived the accident.

'Precious miracle baby,' she whispered, kissing him as he snuggled in her arms.

Her thoughts centred on Gus. Whatever must he be feeling? She glanced at her watch and realised with shock how much time had passed since he'd left the house. Where was he? Fear curled within her. She had to find him. There was so much to talk about, so much to resolve, so many misunderstandings to settle.

First and foremost, she knew how deeply he loved Max. Right now he must be feeling lost, angry and hurt—deceived in the worst of ways. Fresh tears stung her eyes. Her heart was breaking for him. And yet…dared she hope? If it was true that he cared for her, as he'd claimed, then this new development, whilst a devastating shock, freed them from everything that had held her back. She wasn't second best. Gus had never been with Julia.

But even as hope rose it faded again. What if he no longer wanted her or Max now he knew what Julia had done? Scared, confused and sick with worry, she knew she had to find Gus as soon as possible.

Uncaring where he was going, Gus walked the streets, devastated by the discoveries he'd made. It took a moment to realise someone was calling his name, then he saw Seb approaching, with Monty the Labrador walking to heel on a lead beside him.

Seb took one look at him and without a word

ushered him back to the townhouse he shared with Gina—Gina's grandmother, Maria, occupied the attached granny flat. Sitting on the sofa, a mug of tea cupped in his hands, Gus blurted out the whole story, seeing the shock on Seb's and Gina's faces as they learned what Julia had done.

'You need to talk with Holly,' Gina advised when he had finished.

'Whatever I say now will sound as if I'm grasping at anything to hold on to Max,' he argued, a frown etched into his brow as he struggled to come to terms with the knowledge that Max was *not* his son. Nothing before had hurt as much as this.

Gina shook her head, clinging to Seb's hand, a smile forming for the first time. 'You told her how you felt before you found the journal. She told you what concerned her. Think about it. Tell her what you've told us, Gus. I don't think you'll be sorry.'

He wanted to, but he was scared, daunted, riddled with doubts and what-ifs.

The phone rang—a shrill intrusion—and his heart lurched when Gina told him it was Holly. 'She's worried…scared for you. She's been trying to find you. You left your mobile phone at home,' she said, her hand over the mouthpiece.

He listened as Gina reassured Holly. 'Gus is here, hon. Seb found him. We'll bring him home.' Gina paused a moment, glancing at him with a smile of encouragement before continuing. 'You two have a lot to sort out. You need time. Will you let us have Max tonight so you can talk?'

Gus nodded his consent as Gina looked at him in query. Whilst he'd hate being without Max, even for a moment, he knew it was a good idea, and clearly Holly had agreed as Gina ended the call.

Max. His miracle baby. His son…who wasn't *his* son after all. Pain, anger and confusion fought for supremacy. He had no rights whatsoever. Holly was Max's true guardian now. What if she didn't want Gus in either of their lives?

Gus looked terrible. Shell-shocked. Holly wanted to go to him, but she waited until Max and the bag she had packed for him had been handed over to Seb and Gina. It took minutes, yet it seemed a lifetime before the door closed and they were alone.

Tension fizzed in the air. Unable to wait another moment, uncaring that fresh tears were coursing down her cheeks, she wrapped her arms around him.

'I'm sorry, Gus.' Her voice was thick and unsteady. 'So very sorry. I can't understand how Julia could do such a terrible thing to you.'

For a dreadful moment she feared he was going to reject her. Then a pained groan escaped him and his arms encircled her, drawing her tightly against him.

Holly had no idea how long they stood there but she clung to him, absorbing his pain, trying to make sense of all the revelations that had bombarded them in the last hours. Eventually he loosened his hold, drawing back far enough so he could cup her face in his hands, his thumbs gently wiping away the remains of her tears. She saw the glimmer of moisture in his eyes—eyes that were clouded and devoid of their usual life and warmth.

'We need to talk,' she murmured, a knot of nervous tension clenching within her. She had no idea which way this would go.

Gus nodded, taking her hand and leading her

to the living room. They sat side by side on the sofa, the silence building, their fingers twining together as their clasped hands rested on the cushion between them.

'I'm sorry that I allowed myself to be so taken in by Julia and that I let her lies and deceptions override all I had come to know about you,' Gus blurted in a rush, shaking his head, self-derision lacing his husky voice.

'Don't blame yourself, Gus,' she chided gently, hoping to ease the burden he'd unfairly placed on himself. 'I certainly don't. No one knows better than me how clever Julia was at manipulation.'

He swore softly, opening up to her for the first time about the night that should have been their first date. 'I thought you'd stood me up—made a fool of me, rejected me. I waited all the next day for you to apologise, to explain, to say it was a mistake, but I heard nothing and you blanked me when I came back to work. I was gutted. I couldn't believe I'd been so wrong about you, or that I had so misjudged what I'd thought was something special between us.'

'You weren't wrong. I felt the connection the first moment I saw you,' she admitted, feeling the blush that warmed her cheeks, smiling as the clouds began to lift from his eyes and he smiled back. 'Now you know that I had a text from your phone, cancelling. When I heard that you'd been with Julia instead…that she'd stayed the night…'

'A night I had no memory of. Damn it, I *knew* things weren't right. I couldn't understand what had happened, and I knew deep down that I never would have slept with her, but when she came and told me she was pregnant I couldn't take a risk with the baby's life. I insisted on a marriage of convenience to safeguard my rights.'

As he ran the fingers of his free hand through his hair Holly tightened her hold on his other hand. 'I understand. Given your own background, I know you would have done anything to ensure your own child had the things that you missed out on.'

'Yes.' He closed his eyes briefly, before long, dark lashes rose and his gaze clashed with hers. The expression in his smoky green eyes was full of torment. 'But Max isn't my own child, is he?'

'Gus…'

Her throat tightened with emotion. She couldn't bear his distress, and a renewed flash of anger ripped through her at what Julia had done. How had she dared toy with people's lives this way—especially an innocent child's?

'She played us off against each other,' Gus continued in a monotone. 'I think she truly loved Paul. Those later entries showed evidence that she regretted many of the things she had done.'

Holly nodded her agreement, a shiver running down her spine. 'I know what she did to you was unforgivable, but I can't help but be thankful that instinct or conscience got to her and stopped her from aborting the baby.'

'Yes.' He paused, his fingers tightening on hers, his voice husky when he spoke again. 'If you don't want to talk about it I understand, but I'm so very sorry about your own baby. What happened, darling?'

'It was nearly two weeks after I'd split with Euan. I had no idea I was pregnant. I had a terrible pain and was bleeding abnormally, and… and my GP confirmed I'd miscarried,' she finished, her voice catching as she tried hard not to cry again.

'And Julia?'

Gus swore as she told him how her sister had

reacted to the news. 'As she wrote—how ironic that unexpected pregnancy then happened to her,' Holly finished sadly.

'When Julia died everyone was so kind, and I felt so guilty,' Gus confided after a moment. 'I still do.'

'You have no need to,' she reassured him, thinking of her own feelings of guilt and the mixed emotions she had experienced.

'Yes, I do.'

Holly's heart nearly stopped beating when he looked at her and she saw the anguish in his eyes. 'Why?'

'Because I wasn't grieving for a wife I had loved,' he confided, his voice low and raw. 'Do you know what I felt, Holly? Relief. Freedom. Anger that she had risked Max's life. Not that I would ever have wished such a horrible thing to happen to her. But I couldn't tell anyone how I felt—not even you—not without seeming the lowest form of life and admitting all the lies and deceptions.'

'Don't.' She choked out the word. 'You're not the only one, Gus. Truly. I felt relief, too. There were times I hated her, but I didn't want her to

die. She did so many bad things. I tried to preserve the family, but she'd keep throwing everything back in my face. After she betrayed me
with Euan and then cheated me out of the house
I didn't think she could hurt me any more.' She
drew in a shuddering breath and met his gaze,
allowing him to see all that was in her eyes, her
heart, her soul. 'But then she did the worst thing
of all. She took you away from me.'

As Gus drew Holly into his arms and held her,
he wondered if he dared to hope that there might
yet be a future for them.

'Hush, darling,' he soothed her. 'No more tears.
You've cried enough for her. You did all you
could. Neither of us is responsible for her decisions.'

She nodded and gave him watery smile. 'You're
right.'

'So where do we go from here?' he asked after
a moment, fear and uncertainty gripping him.
'I'm not Max's father,' he continued, choking out
the words. 'I have no rights over him. I—'

'Of course you do,' Holly interrupted with
gusto. 'But—'

She wriggled free, and he waited as she sat up and faced him, raising their joined hands and holding them against her heart. 'I know you must be hurting. Julia tricked and deceived you. And I know how much you love Max—and how much he loves you. Any man can father a child, Gus, but it takes a special one to be a loving papa. And you are, in every way that matters, Max's papa.'

'Thank you.'

Her words choked him, and he felt as if he'd been given a precious gift. 'The same way that you are and always will be Max's mama,' he added, smiling at the emotion in her eyes.

What he had not foreseen when he'd found the journal and learned its shocking secrets was how easily the truth would set them free.

'I love you, Holly, my darling,' he told her, praying she would believe him. He drew in a shaky breath and laid his heart on the line once more. 'I want us to be a family, to put the past behind us and make a happy life for us, Max and any other children. You said you felt something for me. Is that in the past tense?'

She shook her head, a shy smile curving her mouth, banishing the last of the shadows from her eyes and thawing any remaining ice inside him. 'I love you, Gus…past, present and future. If you'll let me.'

'Only if you'll let me love you back,' he teased her, joy and relief blooming inside him. 'What do you say? Will you marry me?'

'Yes, please!'

Gus wasn't sure he deserved to be this happy, but he'd been given a second chance and he was going to spend the rest of his life proving to Holly how much he loved her. They'd known so much hurt and loneliness these last months, but now they'd found each other again, and with Max, their miracle baby, they could look forward to a loving and happy future.

EPILOGUE

As HOLLY carefully laid flowers on Julia's grave the late August sunshine glinted off the simple but beautiful aquamarine stone set in the white-gold engagement ring Gus had so recently put on her finger. Her birthstone and, Gus insisted, the colour of her eyes.

He stood beside her, strong and supportive, Max cradled against his chest. They'd had a difficult, often painful journey, but they had come through it and were stronger for it, their love for each other winning out and unable to be denied. Despite all Julia had done.

'Whatever else she did, she gave us Max,' she whispered, hoping that, in death, her troubled sister had found the peace she'd never known in life.

Gus's free arm came round her and she leaned into him. She loved him with every fibre of her being and she knew now that he was hers, that he had never been Julia's in any way. Free of the lies, they could be a proper family.

'Let her go. She can't hurt us any more.' Gus pressed a kiss to the top of her head before stepping back and taking her hand. 'Come with me. I want to show you something.'

Curious, Holly let him lead her back to the car. As he settled Max in his safety seat she reflected on the last few busy days. Days which, amongst other things, had seen Ruth leave for her new life in Italy with Rico. She already missed her friend, but gave thanks that Ruth and Gina were as happy with their respective partners, Rico and Seb, as she now was with Gus. Which left George, she reflected with a smile.

'Oh, that look means trouble!' Gus teased as he slid into the driver's seat. 'What have you been up to?'

Her smile widened to a grin. She wasn't remotely repentant about her spot of matchmaking. One look at the delicious new consultant paediatrician who had begun work on the children's ward had set her mind buzzing. And when she'd discovered he was looking for somewhere to stay, the card George had put on the staff noticeboard advertising rooms to rent had somehow found its way into Rafael's pocket! George hadn't seen him yet, because she was off work on an annual leave, but Holly wished she could see her friend's face when they did meet.

Gus chuckled as she told him what she'd done. 'Did you tell him George was a woman?'

'Oops, I forgot that bit!'

'Your mama is a very bad woman, Maxie,' Gus advised their son solemnly.

Holly's heart swelled with love and happiness. Gus switched on the car's CD-player and the soft, haunting tones of the music he'd composed on the sax and which had so moved her began to play—a piece she now knew he'd composed and named for her. *Holly's Lament*. Joy had replaced the heartache that had inspired it.

When Gus drew the car to a halt, it took a moment for reality to set in. 'What are we doing here?'

Her breath caught as she looked out of the window at the house she loved so much—the one in which she had grown up; the one she had lost because of Julia. Her dream of getting it back had long since turned to dust. She frowned as Gus got out of the car and came round to open her door.

'Gus?'

He took her hand and led her to stand on the wide pavement in the quiet, attractive road. Her eyes widened as she saw the 'For Sale' board fixed to the silver birch tree that stood in front of the house. A 'Sold' sign was pinned across it at a jaunty angle.

'I know what this house means to you. When I found out it was for sale…well, it was destiny,' he told her with a self-conscious smile. He placed a key in her palm. 'This isn't the real key—that will come in a few weeks, when we complete and move in. This is symbolic of my promise to you, of my gift to you—and to Max and me. A special home in which we can raise our family.'

Tears stung her eyes and she threw herself into his arms, laughing and crying at the same time. 'Thank you,' she whispered, although the words seemed inadequate to express her feelings.

This special, wonderful man always surprised her, showing her in endless ways how much he loved her and what their family meant to him.

She was the luckiest woman in the world and she wanted to shout it from the rooftops.

Instead she settled for kissing the man who had made her world complete, and with whom she anticipated living and loving for the rest of their days.

* * * * *

Mills & Boon® Large Print
Medical

October

November

December

Mills & Boon® Large Print Medical

January

SYDNEY HARBOUR HOSPITAL: MARCO'S TEMPTATION — Fiona McArthur

WAKING UP WITH HIS RUNAWAY BRIDE — Louisa George

THE LEGENDARY PLAYBOY SURGEON — Alison Roberts

FALLING FOR HER IMPOSSIBLE BOSS — Alison Roberts

LETTING GO WITH DR RODRIGUEZ — Fiona Lowe

DR TALL, DARK...AND DANGEROUS? — Lynne Marshall

February

SYDNEY HARBOUR HOSPITAL: AVA'S RE-AWAKENING — Carol Marinelli

HOW TO MEND A BROKEN HEART — Amy Andrews

FALLING FOR DR FEARLESS — Lucy Clark

THE NURSE HE SHOULDN'T NOTICE — Susan Carlisle

EVERY BOY'S DREAM DAD — Sue MacKay

RETURN OF THE REBEL SURGEON — Connie Cox

March

HER MOTHERHOOD WISH — Anne Fraser

A BOND BETWEEN STRANGERS — Scarlet Wilson

ONCE A PLAYBOY... — Kate Hardy

CHALLENGING THE NURSE'S RULES — Janice Lynn

THE SHEIKH AND THE SURROGATE MUM — Meredith Webber

TAMED BY HER BROODING BOSS — Joanna Neil